MAGNOLIA

A PERFECT LOVE

ASIA MONIQUE

Copyright © 2024 by Asia Monique

All rights reserved. No part of this book may be reproduced in any form or by any electronic or mechanical means, including information storage and retrieval systems, without written permission from the author, except for the use of brief quotations in a book review.

BLURB

"Lennox spoke to a part of me that no man ever had." — Magnolia

Magnolia Baker could be considered the matriarch of her four younger sisters. They've endured tragedy and heartbreak together, with Magnolia protecting them no matter the cost. Her heart was made of solid gold and under lock and key. Shielding the part of her that had been broken by the one man who should have guarded it with his life is a top priority for Magnolia. No one has ever been able to penetrate the barrier until a smooth-talking college English professor by the name of Lennox Clarke steps in to take a shot.

Does Lennox have what it takes to secure the key to Magnolia's heart, or will his efforts be all for nothing?

INTRODUCTION

Magnolia + Lennox = Love that helped heal.

If you've never read a book by me, then you must know that I write for the people who want to get away from everyday life. If you're looking for drama on every page, then this isn't the book for you. That's it, that's the introduction. With that being said, I hope you enjoy it.
 Xoxo, Asia

WORDS OF AFFIRMATION

Expressing affection through spoken affection, praise, or appreciation.

ONE

MAGNOLIA

What's your love language?

"OK, I'm finished," I said, lifting my head from my phone. My sisters Lilac, Juniper, Daisy, and Blossom were sitting around my kitchen table, each with a different electronic device clutched in their hands or sitting in front of them. I was already aware of my love language, but when Daisy got an email to take a test, she suggested that we do it together.

Lilac lifted her head next and huffed.

"I think this test is stupid, but I'm finished," she said, setting her iPad down and picking up her glass of wine. "Besides, we all know Mag loves to be told she's beautiful."

I flipped her the bird and winked. She hadn't been lying when she said that I love to be told I'm beautiful. I wasn't vain, but I loved compliments, and I love a man who loves to give them. Physical touch was a close second, according to the results of my test, and I agreed with that wholeheartedly. What woman doesn't like to be touched? The thing is if a man could actually *talk* me out of my panties, then they never belonged to me in the first place.

But more importantly, it wasn't all about getting compliments for me. I wanted a man that understood me enough to speak to me in a way that stirred something real inside of me. Something that I'd never felt before.

"Lilac, please hush," Daisy mumbled, her brows furrowed. A few seconds later, she looked up and smiled. "OK, I'm finished."

"Who picked this red wine? I need to add this to the wine list on my blog," Lilac went on, ignoring Daisy. Lilac and I were the oldest of us five, but not by a lot; we were all one year apart. I held the top spot at twenty-nine. With us being so close in age, we bumped heads a little, but it was never anything major. We were best friends and the only family we had left outside of our aunt.

Our mother, Marigold, died from lupus complications a week after my fifteenth birthday. Our father had been out of the household for about six years by that time and completely nonexistent in our lives. When he learned of our mother's death, he did the one thing we hadn't thought he would. He signed over his parental rights, leaving us wards of the state. It hadn't been long before his sister, Lori, found out about what happened and came to get us. Lori was our saving grace, and she took good care of us. We spent our teenage and early adult years living in Brooklyn, New York with her.

We all attended New York University, and after I graduated, I took a job as a marine biologist with a research company here in Philly and made the move. My sisters followed me back to our hometown one by one after graduating and taking jobs of their own.

"I'm done," Juniper and Blossom spoke at once. "Jinx," they both followed up with.

"You guys are so childish," I said, laughing. "Alright, since we already know that my love language is indeed words of affirmation, let's hear your results, Li."

"I think mine may be wrong," she said, frowning. "Acts of service."

"I actually think it matches you well," Blossom chimed, standing from her seat. "Anyone want more wine?"

I handed her my glass, and she sauntered over to the double door fridge to grab a new bottle.

"I agree," Daisy said, nodding. "You prefer someone to show you that they love you, versus them telling you. That's why you and—" Lilac cut an eye at Daisy from across the kitchen, and she quickly shut her mouth. It was an unspoken rule that we not mention her ex-boyfriend by name, or at all for that matter. "OK, Juni, how about you? What do your results say?"

"Receiving gifts," she murmured. She took a sip from the wine glass Lilac had just set in front of her and then added, "I guess I did like when snot-nosed Timmy used to bring me sunflowers covered in dirt back in the day."

Laughing, I asked, "Whatever happened to him?"

"I'm pretty sure he's a doctor now at Penn," she replied. "Daisy, your turn."

"Quality time," we all said, falling into a fit of laughter. Daisy was the reason we had weekly meetups. She was also the reason we had sleepovers once a month like teenagers. We took it all in stride and never complained because truthfully, we enjoyed each other's time.

"I guess we saved the best for last," Blossom chimed in, smiling. "I liked to be touched."

I damn near spit my wine out. "Why'd you have to say it like that?"

She shrugged. "Well, it's true. I love sex, and I love a man's touch." She sipped her wine. "And God knows I've been in a drought for almost a year now, and it's killing me."

"Should the word God be included in that sentence?" Daisy asked, staring at her.

"He knows my heart."

"So, what do we do with this information?" I asked, ignoring Blossom.

"Nothing really," Daisy answered. "I just thought it would be fun."

"Well, it wasn't," Lilac fussed. "Can we order food? I'm starving."

"No," I said. "But you guys can go home and order food to your own places. I have to work in the morning, and I have a phone date tonight." I stood from my seat and eyed each of them.

"What happened to hoes before bros?" Blossom asked. She picked up the empty wine glasses and walked them over to the dishwasher. "I mean, we know Lennox has the gift of gab, but geez, we were here first."

"And you'll be here after him."

"Well, that sounds promising," Juniper quipped, pulling her keys from her purse. "Are you already counting him out?"

I shrugged instead of responding. I didn't want to discuss what I felt or thought about Lennox Clarke. The college English professor from New Jersey whose words made my heart smile.

"Sounds like she's doing what she always does," Lilac murmured as I walked them to the door.

"And what is that?"

"Pushing people away before they hurt you like dad hurt us," she answered simply before leaning in to kiss my cheek. "Like he hurt mom."

"This has nothing to do with dad." I stepped out of my townhome in Logan Square and watched them as they began to pile into their respective vehicles.

"The first step to breaking addiction is admitting you have a problem," Daisy chimed after rolling down her window. "How can you ever be happy if you think every guy will do to you what he did to mom?" She rolled her window up before I could respond and pulled off. I stood outside in the chilly air until each of their cars disappeared off my block.

Sighing, I stepped back into my heated domain and locked myself inside. I set the alarm and retreated to my bedroom for a shower with Lennox on my mind. My sisters had no idea what they were talking about. I didn't push people away because of our sperm donor, I just preferred to protect my heart from hurt. I've experienced enough of it in my twenty-nine years of life, and I'm over the daunting feeling. The thing about Lennox was he was too good with his words. He seemed to always say the right things at the right time. No man was perfect, but he just seemed too good to be true.

Or maybe you aren't giving him a chance to show his imperfections.

I never let it get that far. What was the point?

Once I was in my bedroom, I grabbed my surround sound remote and turned on my shower playlist that consisted of my favorite R&B hits. As Savannah Cristina's song "Self Care" spilled from the speakers, I picked up my phone. My lips tilted up slightly at the sight of Lennox's name.

> Are we still on for tonight?

He'd sent the text twenty minutes ago.

> Of course.

I set my phone down and began to strip out of my clothes. After tossing them into the clothes basket in my closet, I stepped into my en suite bathroom and turned the shower on. Once the temperature was to my liking, I slipped inside and let the hot water coat my skin while my thoughts wandered.

Lennox and I were introduced through my childhood friend Brynlee's husband, Samir. He and Samir grew up together in New Jersey. When Brynlee first came to me about Lennox, I was way more skeptical than I am now. He was a divorcee, and for me, that was a turnoff, but Brynlee swore that I would like him, and she hadn't been wrong.

He was handsome, sweet, and successful. The fact that he taught English at the University of Pennsylvania said a lot to me. I mean, it's an Ivy League school, and he's still young, only just hitting the age of thirty.

So why are you thinking of pushing him away?

I huffed and picked up my favorite rose hemp soap and lathered it into my exfoliating gloves. I scrubbed my skin down, rinsed, and then repeated the steps. When I felt like I was clean, I removed my gloves and grabbed a rag to clean my more sensitive areas. After a few more minutes, I was cutting the water off and reaching for a towel. I had only been able to moisturize my skin before my phone began to ring, with Lennox's name flashing across the screen.

"Hello," I answered, placing him on speaker while I slipped into a pair of leggings and a sports bra.

"Ms. Baker," his smooth tone spoke, giving me chills. "Tell me something."

I smiled. He started every conversation that way. I'd learned over the last couple of months that it was his way to get to know me without asking specific questions.

"Well, my love language was confirmed today."

"Yeah? And what might it be?" I slipped under my blanket and then picked up my phone.

"Words of affirmation."

He chuckled. "I should've known. Your eyes always light up when I tell you how beautiful you are."

"Doesn't every girl's eyes light up when being told that?"

"Some people aren't good at taking compliments, Lia."

Lia.

He'd given me the nickname on our first date, and it just stuck. I loved hearing it more than I'd like to admit.

"I guess I'm one of a kind."

"That you are," he mused.

"OK, it's your turn."

"Alright," he started. "My brother and his wife are pregnant with their sixth child."

"Really!"

"Yeah. I'm not sure if they're excited about it or not. The youngest just turned two."

"I think children are a blessing," I said, thinking of my sisters. Before my mother passed, she handled the five of us beautifully, and it never seemed forced or stressful. "No matter how many."

"I agree with you. I want about five myself."

"Why didn't you and your ex-wife have—never mind."

"Don't do that," he chastised. His tone wasn't harsh, but it was stern enough for me to hear him loud and clear. He didn't want me holding back. "Ask the question."

"Why didn't you guys have kids?"

"She didn't want any, and I respected her wishes."

"But you want five?" I asked.

"I want a big family, and it took being just her and me for so many years for me to realize that."

Interesting.

"Is that why you guys—"

"She cheated." His words came out so smoothly that it took a minute for them to register. "I can tolerate a lot of things, but that's a betrayal I'm not strong enough to take."

"You sound—"

"Like I'm not hurt? Or fazed?"

"Yeah."

"I was at the time, but it's been two years, and I've let go. She's moved on, and so have I."

"You make it sound so easy, Lennox."

He laughed. "If you had met me around the time it happened, then you'd be singing another tune."

"Do you ever wonder why she did it?"

"I know why," he said, sighing. "It's a long story, and not something I want to discuss during one of these calls."

"That's fair."

"How about you let me take you out again?" he continued.

"I don't know," I whispered, turning in bed. The more we hung out, the more my feelings for him grew. That only meant one thing to me. He could possibly hurt me, and I didn't want that.

"I'm getting the feeling that you don't actually want to see me again."

We'd only been on one *real* date. The other times we've seen each other were in passing. A car conversation here and there. But that date, it went so well. The conversation flowed smoothly, and it felt like I'd known him all of my life. That scared me. Another date would mean feeling that way again. I didn't like being scared.

"It's just—"

"Don't worry about it," he said. "Whenever you're ready." He didn't sound upset, but why did his words sting a little?

"OK."

Whenever you're ready.

I had no idea when that would be.

"BAKER, do you have that file from last week's water sample?" Mariana—my research partner—asked after poking her head into my office.

We worked out of a small laboratory and office space near the University of Pennsylvania campus when we weren't out in the field. As Marine Biologist, we studied life in the oceans and the ocean themselves. The most intriguing part of this career was visiting different aquariums and zoos to study their wildlife. It's our job to learn what's out there so we can protect it, while also protecting the people who may come in contact with these species. Instead of working for a government-run agency, we worked out of a private research lab, which gave us more room to do as we pleased. And though it got boring at times, it felt good to be in a career I loved so much.

"I emailed you a copy," I said, looking up from my computer. "I'll be heading down to the lab in a second."

She nodded and said, "I'll meet you down there." I went through a few more emails and then reached for my phone. There were text messages from the group chat with my sisters and a few of our friends. There were also two messages from Lennox. I only had time to look at a few, so I opted to check his.

> Lunch?

I thought about his offer and decided to go for it.

> Is two cool?

> That works. I'll see you at two outside of your building.

I sent him my location and closed out of the thread. He'd been here once before, but I wanted to be sure he had it in case he forgot. I knew his message was his way of letting me know that meeting him at the restaurant was out of the question. And who was I to deny the man his right to pick me up? With a smile on my face, I stashed my phone in my desk drawer and headed down to the lab.

"Why do you seem happier than usual?" Mariana asked after entering the lab.

"I look the same," I said, turning from my station to face her.

"No, you look like something recently happened that has you smiling." She smirked and then tossed on her white lab coat. "Care to share?"

I rolled my eyes and turned in my seat.

"There's nothing to share."

"Fine, be stingy," she said, huffing. "Any lunch plans? I want to get sushi."

"Yeah, I have plans." There was a brief silence, and then a loud hum filled the room. I didn't need to see her face to know what she was thinking. I waited for her to ask more questions, but they never came, and I was appreciative of that. After setting up my station, I put my earbuds in, turned my music up, and got to work.

Two hours later, we were wrapping up the first half of our day and heading out to lunch. I stepped out into the eerily warm air and looked around. It was mid-February, and there was no snow on the ground or blistering winds to show for it. I wasn't complaining, but it had me worried that we would get our winter during the springtime. The sound of a door shutting pulled my attention to the sleek dark gray Mercedes Benz truck. Lennox stepped in front of me, giving me the best view of his blemish-free toffee-colored face. I followed the firm outline of his jaw and then worked my way up.

Have you ever seen a man's eyes match his skin color?

I damn near melted the first time I saw him in person. The saying tall, dark, and handsome was created to describe Lennox. God had blessed him for sure.

"Wassup, beautiful," he said, leaning in to kiss my cheek. "Are you ready?"

He calls me beautiful as if it were a part of my government name. The word always left his lips so effortlessly. There was no thought to it. I was beautiful to him, and that was that.

"Yes, I am starving," I finally answered. He chuckled and guided me to the passenger side door. I wasn't used to a man being such a gentleman with everything they did. He opened my door, and I slipped inside. I reached out to close it, but Lennox handled that for me too. As I put my seatbelt on, I watched his tall, lean frame swagger around to the driver's side. He had this cool demeanor about him that I liked. It was almost as if no one could penetrate that barrier and get him to act out of character. I liked that too.

"I was thinking we could hit Allegro's," he said, placing the car in drive. Allegro's was a popular pizza and grill near campus.

Now was the perfect time to go because it wouldn't be overrun by students. "Is that cool?"

"Perfect."

He nodded and headed in that direction. "I'm glad you agreed to this."

I nodded and asked, "What happened to when I was ready?" I glanced his way and caught the grin that showcased the deep dimple in his right cheek. It was so damn sexy on him.

"Sometimes, all it takes is a little initiative," he replied, giving me a quick look before focusing his gaze on the road. "I want to get to know you more, so I'm putting in the effort to do so."

"So, you figured asking wouldn't harm?"

"And look what that got me," he mused, chuckling.

"A lunch date." I turned my head to hide my smile.

Smooth bastard.

TWO

LENNOX

"Mr. Clarke, I'm trying to get into this book, but it just doesn't interest me," one of my students called out during the questioning part of my lecture. I glanced around the large classroom with stadium-like seating until my eyes landed on one of my best students. I leaned up against my desk and crossed my arms.

They were currently reading *The Grapes of Wrath*. If I were being honest, it wasn't one of my personal favorites, but it was a part of the required curriculum. I did have some pull with said curriculum, though, and could change some things around if needed.

"Who else feels the way Ms. Fredericks does?" I asked, making eye contact with as many students as I could. I taught two English courses. One in the morning and one in the evening on Monday, Wednesday, and Thursday, each held about fifty to sixty students. A slew of hands went into the air, and I nodded. "Alright, so what do you guys want to read?"

"We get to pick?" a few asked, eyes wide.

"Today you do, but here's the thing," I started, uncrossing my arms. I walked over to the whiteboard and picked up a black marker. "If I let you pick, it has to be something from one of these four authors." I wrote Toni Morrison, Charles Dickens, Ralph Ellison, and T.S. Elliot's names on the board.

"Well, I vote Toni Morrison," someone called out from the left side of the room.

"T.S. Elliot has great stuff too," another said. They went on and on like that for a few minutes before I got things in order. I truly enjoyed it when my students engaged with me and each other. It made classes much more interesting.

"Everyone, get out a piece of paper and write down one of the four names on it," I said. "When you're finished, fold it and then pass it up to the front." While they did that, I reached for my phone to check the time. We had about twenty more minutes left before class was over. I set my phone down and went to grab the pile of folded papers. "Did everyone send one down?"

"Now, what happens?" Ms. Fredericks asked after I dropped the pile onto my desk.

"Now," I said, turning around, "you guys go home and enjoy your weekend. I will see you on Monday with the winning author's name and a list of books to choose from. Take care, everyone."

It was Thursday, but this class was full of mostly seniors. If they were anything like me when I was a senior, then they had no classes on Fridays so that they could start their weekends early. As they dispersed, I began to gather my things so that I could head out. I hated taking work home, so I tried doing most of it here, but today, I wanted to get off campus as quickly as possible. With my phone, briefcase, and laptop bag clutched in my hands, I walked out of Bennet Hall toward the parking lot where I'd parked my truck after lunch with Magnolia.

Speaking of Magnolia Baker...

"Ms. Baker, to what do I owe this call?"

"I just wanted to tell you that I enjoyed lunch today."

I was a little surprised she called to say that. Things with Magnolia had been running hot and cold since we first met almost six months ago. When we were just having phone conversations and sending text messages non-stop, everything was smooth, but the moment we met face-to-face, she switched up on me. I had to figure out why.

"Yeah?"

"Yes," she all but whispered. "I was thinking maybe we could do it again?"

Another surprise.

"If I can have you for the entire day, then yes, we can do it again," I said, securing my things in the back seat of my truck. I slid into the driver's seat, and shortly after that, I was pulling onto the road. "So, what do you say, Ms. Baker, can I see you Saturday?"

"That sounds—Juniper, please go home."

"I need a shirt for my night out," her sister whined in the background. "Is that Lennox on the phone? Heyyy, Lennox."

"Please, don't mind her," Magnolia said before I could respond. "I need to get her out of here, but yes, Saturday sounds great."

I confirmed it one more time, and then we hung up. I decided while I headed to my Center City apartment that I would call and check on my older brother. He had me by five years, but the age difference didn't matter. He was my best friend. Growing up, it was just me, him, and our pops.

"Lenny!" his deep voice blared through my truck's speaker. I could hear my nieces and nephews yelling and laughing in the background. Leonard had five kids, all under the age of twelve, and his sixth would be here in five months. He and his wife Tamera had been together since I was fourteen.

"Please don't call me that." I grimaced and gripped the steering wheel tighter than I intended. It was what our mother called me back in the day. She still used the nickname, and though I hated it, I preferred that only she used it.

"My bad," he said. "It's a habit. Wassup?"

"I was calling to check on those badass kids of yours and to see if you told pop yet about the baby."

"I told him a few hours ago, and the nigga laughed." I smirked and shook my head. That sounded like our father. He knew Leonard didn't want more kids, but he also wouldn't stop fucking his wife—who didn't believe in birth control—either. He had to take one or the other. "She's getting her tubes tied, burnt, or whatever they do to them after this one."

"Did you talk her into that?"

"Nah," he said. "She asked the doctor about it at her appointment today, shocking the fuck out of me."

"You don't sound as happy as I thought you would," I pointed out.

"I mean, I want my wife happy, but you know how she feels about altering the body to stop things that are natural. I guess I'm just trying to figure out if she's doing it for me or if it was really her decision."

This was one of the reasons I admired my brother. No matter what he felt about something, he always took his wife's feelings and beliefs into consideration. I tried doing the same in my own failed marriage, but things hadn't worked out good for me.

"Talk to her about it."

"That's the plan."

"Good," I said, pulling into my designated parking spot. "I just got home, but hit me later before my favorite girl goes to bed." He laughed. I knew he was shaking his head, but he promised to call before we disconnected. Leonard's two youngest kids are girls. Kendall is four, and Kaylie—my favorite girl—is two. I was her Godfather, and baby girl understood that. She used the small fact to her advantage every chance she got.

As I entered my two-bedroom luxury apartment, I cut on lights along the way. Though being a professor brought in good money, it wasn't my only source of income. I was able to afford my two thousand square foot apartment because of the two best-selling novels I had written.

It still sounded surreal that I was a New York Times bestselling author. I didn't like to tell many people who I was. It would bring about attention that I didn't like to have. Writing was a passion of mine, but I didn't want the limelight that came with blowing up like I had. I was grateful that keeping my anonymity wasn't a problem. Only my family knew me as a writer and were aware of my pen name. I didn't use the success of my first or second book to get my job at Penn. I simply interviewed as a young man with an English degree from Villanova and a master's from none other than the University of Penn. They jumped at the opportunity to have me.

Moving through my apartment, I walked into the second bedroom that I'd transformed into an office. I deposited all of my things in there and then headed for the kitchen. Prepping dinner was always the first thing I did before getting settled. While moving around the kitchen, my mind went back to the interesting lunch I'd had with Magnolia.

"I'm usually not a big fan of pizza," she murmured, biting into a slice and then groaning. *"But this place makes me change my mind every time I have it."*

"I'm glad my choice of fine dining is up to your standards."

"You've exceeded my expectations," she replied, smiling at me. That smile was everything.

"Tell me something."

"I get to go scuba diving tomorrow." Her eyes lit up, and I laughed.

"The way your face just lit up tells me that's your favorite part of the job."

"It really is," she mused. *"I love being deep in water with different wildlife swimming around me. It's serene."*

"I'd love to do that with you one day."

She sat up straight and eyed me curiously. *"Really?"*

"Yeah, really."

"Well, I'd love for you to join me one day, but only if I can sit in on

one of your classes."

She had me there.

Her wanting to step into my area of expertise made me like her even more. And though I liked her, there was still that small reminder that she was holding back. I wanted to know why, but that was a battle for another day.

I finished prepping the wings I planned on deep frying, washed my hands, and then picked up my phone. I slid through my contacts and stopped on one name that I talked to as much as I could but sometimes fell short on.

"Hey, son," my mother answered. Her voice was raspier than the last time we'd spoken.

"Ma," I said. "How are you?" I could hear her sucking in a breath and then blowing it out, letting me know that she was smoking on the cigarettes she loved so much.

"I'm as good as I can be." That was always her response. I never got more out of her, and I wish I could. "How are you? Do you have a new book coming soon?"

"Not anytime this year, but I'll be back in the game soon." I'd signed a five-book multi-million-dollar deal with Kensington Publishing, and so far, I'd released two of the five. My agent was a gem, and if it weren't for him, I wouldn't have been able to ink the deal on my own. "Ma, can I ask you something?"

"Of course." She didn't sound sure, but then again, she never sounded sure of anything. Sia Clarke suffered from a bad case of post-traumatic stress syndrome. What caused it was simply the life she was forced to live growing up. Her parents—my grandparents—weren't the best, and they allowed some horrible things to happen to her. Things that I refused to repeat. She had managed to find happiness with my father for a little while, but after she had me, it was like she broke, and nothing could fix her. When I was five, she had a psychotic break that landed her in a mental institution. After years of getting better and then slipping back into that dark space, my father—with power of attorney over her medical decisions—made a choice to place her in a group home. I didn't agree with the placement, but he thought the structure was important for her. For the last two years, she seemed to be in a good headspace, but we could never be too sure.

"Do you ever think about being back home with dad?"

It was a question that had been on my mind for the last few weeks. I knew she hated where she was, and my father missed her no matter how hard he tried to act as if he didn't. He feared he wasn't enough for her, and I think she feared that she'd never be who he once thought she was. I, on the other hand, had faith that things would work in both of their favor.

It was all about adjusting.

"I think that sometimes dreams don't come true, Lenny."

And then she ended the call.

I wasn't fazed by the abrupt hang-up. She did it often, and I'd become accustomed to it. Most would say I had a fairytale way of thinking, but that was the furthest thing from the truth. I just had hope. I believed that the tools were there for us to be better. And maybe I'm wrong, but I'd rather live with that being my reality after trying first.

I shook away what I liked to call creative brain—where my thoughts on many different subjects that don't connect in any way take over—and headed to my office to get some work done. I planned on going through the votes from my last class, picking a set of books for them to choose from, and then reading over at least half the papers from my morning class—which was a freshman course.

TWO HOURS LATER, I was deep into grading papers with a plate of half-eaten chicken sitting next to me when my phone began to ring. I glanced at it briefly but then gave it my full attention when I caught the sight of Magnolia's name.

A FaceTime call.

I quickly answered.

"Hey," she chirped, smiling into the camera. Her hair, which she usually wore down and in its naturally curly state, was pulled up into a tight bun, giving me a view of her beautiful deep dark face.

"Two calls in one day," I said. "I'm starting to think you like me more than you let on."

"You think that I don't like you?" she asked, tilting her head. I knew she liked me, but how could I get her to let go of whatever it was that was holding her back if I didn't push a little?

"What I think doesn't matter, Lia. It's about what you show me."

"Tell me what I show you."

"How about you tell me what it is that makes you want to run?"

She averted her gaze.

"I don't want to run, but I also don't want to be hurt," she said. She was now moving through a dark space, and then a few seconds later, she was in my view again. "So, I guess in order for me to not be hurt by people, I run."

"Do you think I'll hurt you?"

"It depends on if you want more than just a friendship with me."

"Friends can hurt their friends."

"I know, but I don't have to be completely open with my friends. I can keep a part of myself to *myself* if that makes sense. If I decided to give my heart to someone, then I have to give all of me without any conditions."

"And that's not something you think you could be open to?"

"I—I don't know, but what I do know as of right now is that I enjoy talking to you. And I really enjoyed your company today too. I like you, Lennox. I just..." She trailed off and sighed.

I can't lie, her response had me feeling a little salty, but I'd learned long ago that you can't force something with someone when it's not what they want.

I liked Magnolia.

A lot.

She's different...

And I like different.

Her aura was always bright, yet once you got to know her, you saw more than what meets the eye. Her spirit was inviting, but she was fighting that trait. If she wasn't comfortable with giving me more of herself, then I would respect that.

"Lennox," she whispered, giving me a thoughtful look. "I'd really like us to be friends for now. I don't know what the future holds, but I need time to figure that out."

I stared into those eyes that turned the lightest shade of brown when the sunlight hit them and thought about how I wanted to handle this.

Did I want to be her friend?

Just her friend...

Or did I want to let her go?

If I wanted a friend, I could call up my ex-wife. She'd been trying since the divorce was final, but I wouldn't budge. I forgave her infidelity, but that was all she would get out of me. If I couldn't be friends with a woman I'd known for ten years, then how could I be friends with a woman who I've known for less time? Even if it felt like a lifetime.

"Yeah, we can try the friend thing," I found myself saying. I was going against everything I believed in, but maybe Magnolia would be worth it.

Or maybe you're wasting your time.

I guess only *time* would tell.

"So then we can still hang Saturday?" Her tone was hopeful.

"Can I still have you for the entire day?" She nodded. "Then we can still hang on Saturday."

"What time should I expect you?"

I thought about the things I could take her to do and then said, "Ten o'clock. Dress comfortably."

THREE

MAGNOLIA
SATURDAY MORNING...

Why was I so nervous?

This wasn't a date.

It is not a date.

"He talked to Samir last night," Brynlee whispered into the phone. "I tried to listen in, but I got shut out."

"Why are you whispering?"

She giggled and then coughed. "Samir is watching me from the living room."

"Girl, don't get in trouble," I joked, walking in front of my wall-length mirror. I was wearing one of the sets from Beyoncé's Ivy Park and Adidas collaboration. The maroon and orange looked amazing against my skin. "Besides, this isn't a date. We're just hanging out as friends."

She snorted.

"I've known you for a long time, Mags," she murmured. "And because of that, I won't tell you what I think just yet."

My doorbell rang, and I checked the time. He was early.

"I think he's here," I whispered.

"Have fun on your date, babe," Brynlee chirped.

"It's not—" The line cut out before I could finish my statement. The doorbell rang again, and I rushed to it. I snatched the door open and came face to face with my baby sister. She pushed past me, and I shut the door to follow behind her.

"What's wrong, Bloss?" I asked, entering my bedroom. She was face first in my mattress. After a few seconds, she lifted her head and gave me the saddest puppy dog eyes I'd ever seen on her. I walked further into my room and sat on the edge of the bed. "Bloss."

"Tell me what this means," she started, rolling over onto her back. "So I met this guy like a month ago, and we went on a few dates." I nodded while picking at her curls. "We talked every single day, texted like crazy, and then he just ghosted me. Is there something wrong with me?"

"No, but there's something wrong with him," I told her, shaking my head. "Any man that ghosts my fine ass baby sister doesn't deserve her. And let me be clear, you aren't just your beauty. Blossom Baker, New York University graduate and public relations professional extraordinaire." We all had amazing careers, but Blossom and Lilac's were the fanciest, in my opinion.

"Don't forget that I was summa cum lade," she added, smiling.

"You were, and that further proves my point."

She nodded and sat up. "You are right. I knew coming here would make me feel better." Blossom looked around my bedroom, and then her eyes roamed my frame. "Wait... It's early. Are you heading somewhere?"

"Yeah, I—" My doorbell rang, and my heart began to race.

This time I knew it was *him*.

"Oh my God," she gasped. "I totally forgot about your friend date." We were walking up the hall as she talked. As we neared the door, she bounced past me and then pulled it open. "Oh, damn..." She turned to look at me. "Is this Lennox?"

None of my sisters had met him yet. They knew of him and saw pictures, but those did him no justice.

"I am," he said, amusement dancing in his dark orbs. "And you are?"

"Oh," she said, turning to face him again. "I'm Blossom, Mags' favorite sister."

"The most annoying one," I mumbled. "Alright, it's time for you to go." I pushed her out the door and pulled Lennox inside. "Drive safe. Love you." I shut the door, turned around, and came face-first with Lennox's chest. "Um..."

"Hey," he said, looking down at me with a boyish smile on his face. "You look..." His eyes moved down my body and then back up to my face. "I want to say sexy, but actually, you look fly as fuck." He looked me over again and nodded. "Yeah, definitely fly."

"Thanks," I said, shying away from him. "I just need to grab my sneakers, and then I'll be ready. There's bottled water in the fridge if you want one."

"I have some water in the truck for us," he said to my retreating back. I held my breath until I was in my bedroom.

"Oh God," I murmured, releasing a deep breath.

His presence was dominating, and he wasn't even trying. I slipped my feet into the solid maroon Ultra Boosts that were also a part of the Ivy Park and Adidas collaboration. The collection had released about a month ago, and I was one of those people that was up and ready with my credit card number memorized. I'd damn near bought every piece.

I made my way downstairs after a few more deep breaths.

"OK, I'm ready."

Lennox turned to face me and smiled. He glanced over his shoulder at the picture he was staring at and then said, "Are those the rest of the infamous flower sisters?"

I laughed. Only a certain group of people called us that, and when I'd told him the story of how we'd gotten the nickname, he started calling us that too.

"Yeah, those are my babies," I said, grabbing my jacket, keys, and bag. We walked out of my townhome and retreated to his truck after I locked the door. Lennox helped me into the front seat as he always did and then shut the door. He was opening the driver's door and sliding inside seconds later. "So, where are we going?"

"Well," he started, snapping his seatbelt into place. "Breakfast first."

"I could eat." I'd skipped the most important meal of the day because I was nervous about spending today with him, so I was grateful that food was the first thing on the agenda.

"There's this spot on Girard Avenue I want to try."

"Ooooh, Green Eggs Café." I bounced in my seat, and he chuckled.

"That's the place," he confirmed. "Have you been there?"

"No, but I saw it on—"

"*Diners, Drive-in, and Dives.*"

"Yes!" I exclaimed. "You watch?"

"It's one of my late-night television show obsessions."

"Lilac, my sister, she's a private chef, but she also has this popular food blog, and she did a piece on them. She raved about the food, so I know it's good."

"What do your other sisters do?" he asked.

I smiled.

I liked that he was trying to center the conversation on a subject that was comfortable for me. He'd gained a couple of points—I didn't know I was collecting—for doing so.

"Well," I said, "Juniper is a music therapist. It's pretty dope what she does for adults and children who suffer from depression or things like autism."

"That is dope."

"Yeah, and Daisy owns a flower shop." I chuckled and shook my head. "She's a florist. I have to remember to call her that or she'll have a fit. Then there's Blossom, who you met, she's a public relations manager at a firm downtown." We also owned a popular clothing boutique collectively, but that was something we didn't bring up often to people. It was called Baker's Clothing

Bar. We dedicated our efforts to styling clients right within our store. It was pretty dope and doing so well that we didn't have to be there as often as we used to. We each spent one day out of the week there to make sure it continued to run smoothly.

"And you all graduated from NYU, right?"

"Yes, where did you go?"

"Villanova for undergrad and UPenn for graduate." I glanced his way with a smirk on my face.

"A double degree man, nice." The conversation continued to flow with ease the entire ride. I was so deep into what he was telling me about his students that I hadn't realized we'd made it to our destination. A couple of minutes later, we were being seated near the back of the restaurant.

"What should we try?" he asked, staring down at his menu. I took a minute to take him in. He had a fresh cut and was looking more handsome than usual. The black and gold-rimmed glasses he wore framed his face just right. He bit down on his lip, and that one dimple made an appearance. "Magnolia?"

"Mmm," I hummed, meeting his gaze. He smirked.

"What should we try?"

"Oh." I looked down at the menu to hide my smile. "Well, Lilac said everything was good, so I think we should get something different so we can try each other's dish."

"She tried everything?" He didn't sound convinced.

"She has this thing where she can't judge a place based on one or two things on the menu. So she tries small samples of each," I clarified, shrugging. "But let's be clear, the girl can eat."

"What about you?" He leaned back in his seat and crossed his arms. "Can you eat?"

Can you?

"I always have a pretty good appetite," I answered, pushing back my dirty thoughts.

"Yeah, me too." Something flashed in his eyes, but it was gone too fast for me to read. "I'll try just about anything once."

"Oh, yeah?"

He nodded and pointed to my menu. "Choose your meal."

Thank God he redirected us because the conversation was slowly going in another direction, whether we wanted it to or not.

"Creole shrimp and grits," I blurted, licking my lips.

He looked up at me and smiled before saying, "Salted caramel banana stuffed French toast."

"That sounds amazing."

"I had a feeling you liked sweet things," he murmured, closing his menu. Our waiter conveniently popped up at our table seconds later with our drinks. He sat them in front of us and then pulled out his pad and pen. I watched Lennox closely as the waiter took down our orders. It probably seemed rude that I'd spoken with my eyes trained on my breakfast companion, but I couldn't look away.

"Why do you think I like sweet things?" I asked as soon as the waiter walked away.

"Everyone has a guilty pleasure."

"Yeah, but how do you know that sweets are mine?"

He shrugged. "I'm good at reading people," he said. "And you give me 'I eat honey buns for breakfast' vibes."

I threw my head back and laughed. "You have no idea how right you are." The wait for our food was spent with me showing Lennox the blog piece Lilac had done on this place.

"She's very detailed."

"I'll make sure to tell her you said that. She prides herself on helping her readers experience the dishes with her." He opened his mouth to speak, but our waiter was back with steaming food on the tray he was carrying. He set our plates in front of us and then bowed out.

"Wow," I gasped, staring down at my bowl of shrimp and grits. "I can smell the spices, and these shrimp are huge." I glanced over the syrupy mess that was on Lennox's plate and licked my lips.

"Shall we switch?" he asked, smirking at me. He'd caught me

drooling, but I wasn't embarrassed. I looked between our dishes and then decided to do something that was against everything I was trying to avoid. Picking up my fork, I scooped up a good portion of the grits and then placed one of the shrimp on top. I looked up at Lennox to find him staring at me curiously.

"So...let's do a trade." I held my fork out and grinned. Before taking a bite of what I offered, he forked some of his French toast and held it toward my lips. We leaned forward at the same time. With our eyes trained on each other, we wrapped our lips around the forks. The flavors from the French toast burst in my mouth, and I felt an orgasm building.

What the fuck?

"Oh my God," I moaned, licking my lips to grab the excess syrup.

"Yeah, that right there is good as hell." He had the utensil I'd just had in my mouth pointed at my bowl. "Good choice."

"That..." I paused and pointed to his French toast. "Was amazing." There was a moment where we just stared at each other. My thoughts were all over the place. How could I only be friends with this man? Lilac was right. Food will bring you closer to someone and make you horny all at once. Eventually, we dug into our own meals and kept up light conversation. The last thing I said to him was, "Where are we going?" He didn't respond. All I got was a wink and then a dimpled smile.

I am in trouble.

"SERIOUSLY?" I screeched. "Lennox!"

"What?" he asked, grinning as he helped me out of his truck.

He'd driven us an hour outside of the city to Hershey, Pennsylvania, where one of my favorite amusement parks was located. Hershey-freaking-park.

"Who told you?"

"Told me what?" he asked, glancing my way as we walked toward the entrance.

"Someone had to have told you that I love this park. Was it Samir?"

He didn't respond as we moved through the line. Once he handed over our tickets and we got our wrist bands, he turned to face me.

"It wasn't anyone," he answered, grabbing my hand and pulling me along. "I told you I'm good at reading people, and I figured you'd enjoy being a kid for one day." I couldn't stop the smile that spread across my face.

Why'd he have to be so good at this?

"I think you may be right."

I didn't get to do things like this often, so the fact that this is what he'd thought up for us to do during this outing made me extremely happy. My smile was big and bright throughout the entire adventure.

A few hours later, we were on the road heading back to Philly. My mind was still reeling from the day. Lennox made me feel so comfortable and at ease the entire time. I didn't feel the need to have my phone out or to do anything that would take my attention away from the moment we were sharing together.

"Did you enjoy yourself?" Lennox asked. I briefly looked his way and then focused my attention on the road.

"I did. It was the most fun I'd had in a while with..." I let my words trail.

"With?"

"A man," I whispered.

"And why is that, Ms. Baker?"

"Tell me something," I said, hoping he'd go with the subject change. Our day went great, and I didn't want to talk about things that put me in a sour mood.

"I like you," he replied. "I think you're dope as hell and beautiful. Smart as fuck, too."

"Do you teach your students with that mouth?"

"I do," he admitted, laughing. "That's why they love me."

"What's the curriculum like these days?"

"Right now, my seniors are...well, were reading The Wrath of Grapes." I turned slightly in my seat to face him.

"Were?"

"Yea, they weren't feeling it, so I let them vote between four authors, and then I'll pick a few books from that author and let them choose what they'll be reading this semester."

"Okay, don't stop there, who are the authors?"

I loved a good book. Words were everything to me. He called out the famous authors' names, and I smiled.

"Do you want to know who won?"

"I really do!" I bounced in my seat like a schoolgirl. "I might have to pick the book up if they choose something I haven't read before."

"It was close between T.S. Elliot and Toni Morrison," he started, glancing my way. "But Toni won out by one vote."

"Really?"

"Yea. I can't lie, I was shocked because my class doesn't hold a lot of Black students."

"You have to tell me which book they choose."

"I will." Our eyes met briefly, and the spark I'd been feeling throughout this day was still there.

"So if this isn't a book that they can get from the school bookstore, then what happens?" I had so many questions.

"I'm going to purchase them all." He said it so nonchalantly that it hadn't registered until he added, "If I want them to be engaged, then I have to invest." That statement alone had me seeing him in a different light. You don't usually hear professors investing in their classrooms in that way. Universities were usually good at providing all that a professor would need, but anything extra would fall on them. Because of that, most followed the curriculum by the book, and that's it.

"How many students are in this class?"

"About fifty." I nodded.

"That's actually a pretty small class, but if you do this often, how exactly are you affording it? I mean, do they pay well at Ivy League schools?"

"They pay us well." His answer was simple, but man, did it leave me with more questions.

Who exactly is Lennox Clarke?

FOUR

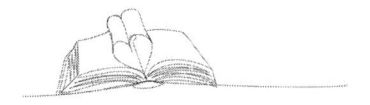

LENNOX

"Good morning," I spoke to each student as they poured into the lecture hall. "Please drop those essays on my desk before you sit down. You know the drill."

"But Mr. Clarke, what if we need to get them out of our bags?" I peered up at the student standing in front of my desk as he reached inside of his bag and pulled out his essay. I leaned back in my seat and crossed my arms.

"I think you've figured out a way around that," I said, lifting an eyebrow. He gave me a silly smile and then turned to head to his seat. I picked up his paper and skimmed it. "Mr. Simmons?" He lifted his gaze to meet mine before sitting. "Is this your best work?"

"It's better than my best," he offered. "Sure of that." I gave him a nod, and he took his seat.

"We have two minutes before class starts. If your paper isn't on my desk by the time we get started, then I don't know what to tell you." That statement earned a few groans, but I wasn't bothered by that. I was harder on my freshmen than I was my seniors. It was a rite of passage, and when the few English or creative writing majors end up in my advanced class a few years from now, they'll appreciate it.

"Um, Mr. Clarke, can I get an extension?"

"Regina Wells, right?" She nodded. There was this deep sadness in her eyes that pulled at my heartstrings. "You have until next class." I understood what it was like to be dealing with personal issues while going to school. I prided myself on being fair but also understanding.

"Thank you, I really appreciate it." I nodded, and she took her seat right at the front as always.

"Who's ready for a lecture!" I yelled, standing from my seat with a broad smile on my face. The chorus of moans and groans I received made me happy.

I was forty minutes into my two-hour lecture when the door to the lecture hall opened, and my ex-wife entered. She gave me a small smile and then took an empty seat in the second row. I gave her one last glance and then continued on with my lesson.

"YOU'VE GOTTEN BETTER," Nina murmured, standing beside me. "They were eating up everything you said." As the last student wandered out of the room, she stepped in front of me. "Hi."

I looked down at who used to be the love of my life and frowned. She was still as beautiful and put together as the day I'd met her. I couldn't stop myself from looking her over a few times.

"Why are you here?" I asked, stepping back slightly. Her head flew up, and those perfectly straightened shoulder-length strands of hers moved with the action. She tucked her hair behind her ear and peered up at me.

"We haven't talked in a while, and I was hoping that maybe we could...you know, *talk*."

"And cornering me at work was your way of getting me to do that?"

"You have to eat, right?"

I chuckled and picked up my laptop bag. "Yeah, but not with you, Nina." She followed me out of the room and then the building. "Look..." I turned to face her as we approached my truck. "I told you a year ago that I've forgiven you. What more do you want from me?"

"I want my friend back," she whispered. "Is that so much to ask?"

"Was it so much to ask you to be honest with your *friend* when you decided that *this* wasn't enough for you anymore?"

"I—"

"Nina... I forgive you, I promise I do, but my forgiveness does not mean that we go back to how things used to be. It just means I'm man enough to own up to my part in the demise of us."

"But—"

"There are no buts. There is no us. We are two people who had a good run and are now moving on with their lives. Please respect my wishes." I leaned in to kiss her forehead and then stopped myself. Instead, I gave her one last glance and then left her standing in the parking lot while I pulled away.

Nina had been trying her hardest to get me to have lunch, dinner... hell, even breakfast with her for a long time. I didn't understand why she was so adamant about us staying friends. She'd cheated and was still with the man who she cheated on me with.

Yeah, we had history, but even that wasn't enough. It would never be enough to make me sit at a table with her and discuss how our new lives were going.

"Yes, Nina?" I spoke after her call flashed across my dashboard.

"I— Um, I've been trying to tell you something, and since you won't sit down with me, then I'll tell you over the phone." I stayed silent, and she smacked her lips. "I'm getting married."

"Why do I need to know that?" I asked, laughing. Who did

this woman think she was fooling? I knew Nina like the back of my hand. "What is it that you really want to tell me?"

"I hate the stupid man, Lenny," she said, chuckling. "I'm sorry I'm such a pest, but he and I don't connect like you and I did, and I guess I wanted some intellectual conversation for a moment."

"If you hate him, then why are you marrying him?"

"Because I'm pregnant."

She'd whispered the confession, but I heard her loud and clear. Nina had been clear when she told me that she didn't want children. It was a little late because we were already married, but being the man that I am, I respected her wishes. Her pregnancy was a shock. A big one.

"I hope you figure that out."

"I'm keeping it."

"I didn't ask."

"But I'm telling you so that you don't hear it from someone else."

"And I appreciate that. Is there anything else you'd like to reveal?"

She laughed.

"No, but if you ever want to get—"

"My answer will always be the same." I had a feeling she understood me this time. "I have another call coming through."

I was guilty of lying to get off the phone, but she would keep me longer if I hadn't. I ended the call and turned my radio up. I needed to drown out where my thoughts were taking me. But even as J. Cole's live *Forest Hills Drive* album blared through the speakers, I couldn't stop the conversation that had changed everything between Nina and me from replaying in my mind.

"*When did you decide that kids weren't on the agenda for you?*" *I asked, staring at my wife of three years.*

"*Well... I told you back when we met that—*"

"*We met in college, Nina. I didn't think...*"

"I was serious. I don't have that want for them like other women." Her eyes filled with tears and fear. The fear of losing me.

I'd pulled her body into my arms and made promises that we would be okay, but the truth was I hadn't been so sure. I never voiced those things to her, and eventually, I began to pull away without realizing that I'd been doing it. Nina sought comfort in another man, and though it hurt like hell to find out that she'd given what belonged to me to another, I had to reevaluate myself. What had I done to push her away? It became clear right before the divorce was final that I'd given up on us, and she felt it. I owned that and cut my losses because though I was a man about my shit, I could never look at her the same. She wanted to fight for us, but that wasn't an option for me. In the end, splitting up was the best decision for both of us.

I pulled my truck into the parking lot of Magnolia's job, parked, and then grabbed my phone to call her.

"Hey, you," she answered. I could hear the smile in her voice. "How was your first class?"

"It was...interesting," I mused. "Can I tell you about it over lunch?"

"Uh...lunch?" She sounded unsure. I sat up in my seat and looked around the parking lot.

"Yeah, lunch. Are you at work?"

"Yes... We are kind of busy." I looked around the parking lot again to make sure that I hadn't missed her car. "But...I can swing lunch. I just texted you an address to meet me at; when you get here, hit the buzzer outside of the door. Bring something fried." After we ended the call, I checked her message and then input it into my GPS system. I knew a chicken spot that was near and decided to stop there on the way.

About forty-five minutes later, I pulled my truck into a spot near a storefront in Center City. As I exited, I eyed the black sign covered in gold lettering that read *Baker's Clothing Bar*. I hit the buzzer as instructed, and when a clicking noise sounded, I pulled the door open.

When I entered the building, I was met with Magnolia's smiling face.

"Welcome," she said, holding both arms out. "I know this is—"

"You own this?" I asked, glancing around at the racks and shelves covered in clothing. The place had a black and gold theme, just like the sign outside. There were couches stationed throughout and other furniture that wouldn't normally be inside of a clothing store. Toward the back, there was a black velvet curtain blocking whatever was behind it.

"My sisters and I do, yes." She began to walk, and I followed behind her. "We each work here one day a week, and this is my day." We stepped behind the black curtain, and I looked around in fucking awe. The backroom was a complete contrast to the front.

"Lia, this is—"

"Unique," she finished, spinning to look at me. "I know. So upfront is set up like a boutique, and then back here is a series of dressing rooms where stylists and designers can come with their clients. We have some in-house stylists, and we also charge a rental fee for anyone who wants to use the space that doesn't work here." We walked further into the space and then into an office. "So, what do you think?"

"I think you're fucking brilliant," I said, stepping closer to the desk and setting the bags in my hands down. "This spot is mad dope."

"It wasn't just my idea," she murmured, plopping down in one of the seats in front of the desk. I took the one next to her.

Reaching over, I grabbed her hand and said, "Yea, I find that hard to believe."

"What do you—"

"I think that this place is your baby, and you put more work into it than anyone else." She gave me wide eyes and then looked away. That was all the answer I needed.

"So, did you bring something fried?" The obvious attempt to

change the subject didn't elude me, but I let her slide. As bad as I wanted to know more about her...to get closer to her, I wouldn't push. Never will I push. Instead, I popped open the container of fried chicken, macaroni and cheese, and string beans, then slid it her way.

"You're a godsend."

"I take it you haven't eaten today?"

She shook her head as she stuffed her mouth with a forkful of mac and cheese. "No, it's been crazy here, and I like to help out when the girls are busy."

"Hands-on," I mumbled. "I like that."

"So," she blurted. "Tell me why class was interesting today."

I took time to eat a piece of chicken and dig into my sides before responding. I felt Magnolia's eyes on me, but I ignored her.

Once I got my fill, I turned to her and asked, "We're trying this friend thing out for real, right?"

"Yes," she answered immediately. I liked that there wasn't any hesitation in responding. She was sure of her choice in us just being friends. I can't lie, it was also slightly disappointing, but I'd already agreed, and backing out wasn't an option.

I nodded and said, "My ex-wife came to visit me during my lecture."

FIVE

MAGNOLIA

Why did hearing that his ex-wife visited him make me want to fight?

I gripped my fork while stabbing at my food. *What the hell is wrong with me?*

"Are you okay?"

"So she came all that way to tell you that she was getting married?" I asked, ignoring his question. There was no way I could answer that without outing myself.

Lennox leaned back in his seat and crossed his arms. I was beginning to notice that the gesture was his signature move. His eyes were trained intently on me before he chuckled and looked away.

"She also came to tell me that she's pregnant."

"Excuse me?" I cocked my head to the side while he gave me a *this isn't a joke* look. "I thought she didn't want kids."

"That was my understanding," he said, closing the container on his half-eaten lunch and then placing his gorgeous eyes on me. "My morning was something else."

"Are you... How do you feel about her being pregnant?"

"I'm not sure I feel anything about it." He shrugged. "Do you think that's normal?"

"I think that people are good at making themselves feel nothing even when they do. Is that normal? No, but it's our way of protecting ourselves."

There was a brief silence before he hit me with, "What are you protecting yourself from?"

"I—"

My office door flew open, and one of my employees poked her head inside.

"I'm sorry, Magnolia, but the Henson bridal party is here." She gave me a pleading look, and I laughed.

"Let her know that I'll be handling her group today."

"Thank you," she said, smiling. "You're the best." She shut the door quietly, and I returned my attention back to Lennox. Jennifer had no idea how grateful I was for her interruption.

"So—"

"Our lunch is over," he said. He glanced down at his watch and then back at me. "I need to get back to campus myself." Lennox stood and then grabbed my hand to pull me up. As his arms wrapped around my waist and pulled me close, I sucked in a breath. His touch was a chaser for the words that left his lips next.

"You fear me for some reason, but I'm not here to hurt you, Lia."

I couldn't even look him in the eye and deny what he'd just said. It was true, I feared him. Instead of speaking, I leaned into the kiss he laid on my forehead and then walked him out. As I watched his truck pull away, I felt my heart tugging me in his direction. That feeling was a shock to my system because I'd never felt it before, and I had no idea what it meant.

"Boss lady, is that your boyfriend?" Jennifer asked while the rest of the ladies stood around gawking at me.

"He's a friend," I said. They all gave me knowing looks, and I rolled my eyes. "Get back to work, or I'll give the Henson party to one of you." The threat was enough to send them scattering around the store. Before slipping behind the black curtain, I took a deep breath, plastered the brightest smile I could muster up on my face, and then went to work.

"Ms. Henson, I think I have the perfect reception dress for you." The bride-to-be, who was a spoiled brat, smiled broadly and followed me to the dressing room that was already set up for her.

I tried my best to keep Lennox off my mind while I worked the rest of the day, but the task was a hard one. As I let the last employee out through the back of the store that night, he was still on my mind. I was currently sitting behind my desk, going over paperwork from the day, when my phone rang. I glanced at the screen and smiled.

"Hey, pregnant lady," I cooed.

"Oh, please, not you too," Nova groaned. "Even Noah is calling me that now."

"He's just doing it to annoy you." Nova was one of my best friends from high school. She's one of the sweetest beings I'd ever encountered, and at that time in my life, I needed someone like her. She had no idea how much her lively, yet calm personality saved me from myself. "How's the baby?" Nova was almost four months pregnant.

"Ugh, making me so sick, Mags."

"Poor baby, do you need anything?"

I knew she was pouting as she said, "Well, I really want a cheesesteak, but Elijah won't let me make the trip to Philly."

"That sounds like your loving but overprotective husband." She laughed, and it made me smile. "How about you talk Brynlee into coming down with you? You guys can stay at my place, and we can make a weekend of it."

"I thought you'd never ask," she said. "See, Bryn, I told you she'd suggest it."

"You could have asked before she had to!" Brynlee yelled from the background.

"How about this weekend? The guys will be in Jersey."

"This weekend sounds like a plan." I looked at the receipts

scattered over my desk and decided to let Lilac deal with them tomorrow. "Is Elena coming too?"

"I'll be there," Elena's soft voice chimed in. I laughed. I should've known they were all together.

"Great." I began to clean up the mess on the desk as I added, "Well, ladies, I have to go. I'm closing up the store." I could hear Elena whispering in the background, and Brynlee explaining that we have a clothing store. "I'll give you a tour this weekend, Elena."

"Okay, I really feel a part of the family now," she said, laughing.

"Mags, we'll let you go. Be safe," Nova said before ending the call.

I smiled at the thought of having the three of them in Philly this weekend. I needed advice, and my best girls always gave the *best* advice.

"LET ME GET THIS STRAIGHT," Daisy murmured into the phone. "He told you about his ex-wife, and you got jealous."

"I didn't get jealous," I argued.

"But you felt a way."

"I felt... Okay, I felt jealous."

"Thanks for admitting that because I am in a really chill mood right now, and getting you to open up takes a lot of energy."

"What does that mean?"

"It just means that you're closed off to everyone."

"I'm only closed off to—"

"Everyone, Mags," she said, cutting me off. "We don't take it personally, but it's true."

"I— I'm sorry."

"I'm not telling you that to get an apology. We all have our ways to deal with how dad fucked us up, and yours is to protect yourself in the fiercest way possible."

"By holding people at arm's length."

"And for the record, you open up to us, it's just on your own time."

"What should I do about Lennox?"

I like him. I think he's as genuine as they come, and he makes me smile.

That's the best part. *He makes me smile.* My heart sputters when he's around.

Being his friend was my way of closing him out, but maybe I didn't really want that.

"Honestly, I think you need to face your fears, and I don't mean with Lennox."

"You mean—"

"We need to face dad."

"We?"

"Of course, did you think I'd let you do it alone?" she asked. "And once the girls find out, they will want to face this with you as well. We're all just as damaged by that stupid nigga."

"Daisy!" She laughed, and I couldn't help but laugh with her. Daisy was more quiet and reserved than the rest of us. She barely cursed, and she despised the N-word.

"Well, he is stupid, and he deserves to be called that God-forsaken word."

"Ain't that the truth," I mumbled. "I love you, Dais."

"I love you more, Mags. Call me tomorrow morning." We ended the call, and I stretched out on my oversized sectional.

I'd never considered reaching out to my father. Not once. My main goal had always been protecting my sisters from the bullshit that transpired after our mother passed. Her job had become mine. I took the brunt of the hurt, so they didn't have to. Even when our aunt took us in, I was still a mother figure to my sisters. Lori did what needed to be done, but I never wanted her to feel like we were too much. I made sure the girls did their homework, chores, and stayed on the straight and narrow.

To their defense, they didn't need much guidance when it came to those things. We knew what was at stake. We knew that Lori could give us back if she wanted. She could ship us off to foster care and be done with us at any time. After a while, we realized that she'd never do that. Nope, Lori loved us as if we were her own, and I know my mother was in heaven grateful that someone had stepped up. Thinking of my aunt made me want to talk to her, so I picked up my phone and called.

"Well, if it isn't my oldest baby," she answered. Her voice was so soothing and inviting.

"Hey, auntie. I miss you."

"I miss you and your sisters more," she said. "When do I get to see you?"

Lori still lived in Brooklyn. She declined moving back to Philly when we asked her, and though I wanted to fight harder on the matter, I didn't. She'd left Philadelphia a couple years before I was born, and moving back just wasn't an option for her. Still, always visited for our sake.

"How about you come to host a girl's weekend?"

"As in come cook and clean up after you, your sisters, and friends."

"No!" I exclaimed. "You are not our maid, but if you'd like to cook for us, we won't deny you that right."

"Mmm. You aren't as slick as you used to be, Magnolia Baker."

"Nova will be here," I continued. "You know she's pregnant. Brynlee is coming, and she's planning a summer wedding. Also, Elena—"

"Alright, alright," she cut in, laughing. "Are we talking about this weekend?"

"Yes, but I was hoping you'd come down on Thursday." She was quiet for a little, but I could hear the television going in her background. I knew my aunt well enough to know that she was waiting for me to continue. "I wanted to, um... I wanted to talk to you about my dad."

"We've finally gotten to this stage," she murmured.

"What stage?" I asked, standing from the couch to walk into the kitchen.

"The one where you realize you have questions that need answering."

"I-I think I want to reach out to him." Saying the words made me feel sick. Why did I want to meet with a man who abandoned his five daughters at the worse time of their lives? We'd just lost our mother, for God's sake. In reality, we'd lost both parents in the span of two weeks.

"Well, I'll be there for every step, and I'll see you Thursday afternoon." There was that soothing voice again. "You know, Magnolia, you're just as strong as your mother, and she would be proud of you.... Of your sisters."

My heart felt heavy when she spoke that declaration. Not heavy in a bad way. No, it was full of the love from a woman I miss so damn much.

I missed my mother so fucking much.

The void of her being gone could never be filled, but having Lori eased that pain a little.

"I really hope that's true, auntie, I really do."

"Trust me when I tell you," she said. "It's as true as the sun rising and setting each day."

And I believed her.

SIX

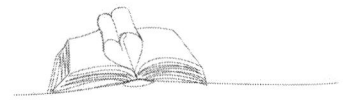

LENNOX

"You've been staring at that phone since you got here," Leonard, my brother, pointed out. "Who is she?"

I ignored him and continued to type out a text to Magnolia.

> Tell me something else...

> I just told you that my home is overrun by my bossy friends and aunt.

> I didn't ask about any of them. I asked about you.

> This weekend and every day after will be life-changing for me.

I stared at that message for a while and then sent:

> How so?

Instead of waiting for a response, I closed out of our text thread and focused my attention on my nosy ass brother, who was now leaning over my shoulder.

"Magnolia?" he questioned, rounding the island with his daughter Kendall in his arms.

"Daddy, Magnolia is a flower," she said, nodding animatedly. The colorful beads on the ends of her neatly braided hair beat against each other with each movement.

"I know, baby love," he replied, sitting her on the counter. "So, who is she?" His eyes were on me now.

"There are lots of different flowers, did you know that, Uncle Lenny?" Kendall continued. I cringed at being called Lenny, but I never corrected my niece. She wouldn't understand why I hated the nickname, so I let her call me whatever she wanted. "Mommy loves pink roses, but there are red roses and black ones too."

"Kenny, how about you go find your brother and bother him?" he suggested, setting her on her feet.

"Which brother, daddy?" I covered my mouth to stop from laughing. She had her head tilted to the side while she waited for him to answer.

"Doesn't matter." He waved her off, and she took off running, yelling Cory's—the eldest—name. He waited until she was out of sight and then turned to face me. "Alright, who is Magnolia?"

"A—"

"Someone who friend-zoned him," Samir interjected as he entered the kitchen with Elijah and Noah in tow. "Wassup, Nard?"

"Not shit," Leonard replied, slapping hands with him, and then doing the same with Elijah and Noah. He was familiar with Samir because we grew up together. When Samir's brother Semaj invited us to one of his games last season, he was introduced to Elijah and Noah. "Just playing daddy daycare for the day while the wife is out." After finishing his statement, he paused and furrowed his brows. "Which kid let y'all in?"

"Ashton," Elijah answered.

"Ashton, what did I tell you about opening the door without

your mother being with you or me?" he yelled, exiting the kitchen.

"I don't see how he can keep up with all those kids," Noah said, grimacing. "I want like two, but I can't do more than that." Elijah snorted, and Noah cut him a wary eye. He was dating Elijah's sister Elena. The connection between everyone was unique, but I appreciated the close-knit group. It had a nice family feel to it.

"Alright," Leonard started, reentering the kitchen with my godbaby attached to his leg. He was walking as if she wasn't even there, which made it evident that he was used to it. "How did you get friend-zoned?"

I shrugged. "She wants to be friends." That was the simplest way for me to put it.

"But you don't."

I shrugged again. "I'm cool with whatever."

I didn't like the way I felt when I said those words. It mattered to me. More than I wanted to admit.

"I don't believe you," Leonard mused, eyeing me curiously. "But we can discuss that another time."

"On to the important matter at hand," I said, grinning at Elijah and Samir. Elijah didn't have a bachelor party because his wedding was planned in such a short time. Samir got married without anyone knowing, so we needed to make up for both occasions. He and Brynlee were having an actual wedding this upcoming summer. The plan was to celebrate both he and Elijah during the bachelor party. I wasn't into strippers, but I would take one for the team.

They glanced at each other, then both said, "No strippers!"

"But strippers are—"

"Don't get beat the hell up," Tamera yelled, cutting Leonard off. She didn't even stop to speak. All I caught was the back of her long hair, and then she was out of sight.

"It's good to see you too, sis-in-law!" I shouted.

"Now about these strippers..." Leonard whispered.

"No strippers!" That was Tamera's voice again.

"Does she have superhuman hearing or something?" Noah asked.

"When you have a tribe of kids, man, everything is heightened." Leonard shook his head, and we fell out laughing. He looked disappointed, but he would get over it. This was not a celebration of their last days being single, anyway. Not only were they already married, but I didn't believe in that. In my opinion, a bachelor party should be about celebrating a big change in one's life, and that's how it would be planned.

"I BOUGHT YOU SOME THINGS." I handed my mother the bags from Walmart and Target. There were a few different things in them, and she went through each bag, pulling out what was inside one by one. "And this is for your spot in the snack pantry out there."

She glanced up and smiled. "Did you get me chocolate?" she asked, reaching for the bag of sweets.

I nodded. "All of your faves."

"You always take care of me." She stood from her spot on the full-sized bed and walked over to the closet. I watched her for a few seconds and laughed. She was trying to hide the bag of snacks on the top shelf but was too short to reach the area she wanted it in.

"Leonard does, too," I said, standing to help her. "Why are you hiding them?"

"They're haters," she fussed. "Always trying to eat my things while calling me spoiled. They say I don't belong here because I have a good family that takes care of me."

"Has dad been by?" I asked, moving the conversation along. I didn't like it when she said things like that. It made me feel bad that she was living in this group home, but the decision wasn't mine to make. It was my father's, and he felt this was best for her. I personally thought he was scared that he wouldn't be able to take care of her properly. His fear was a valid one, but I planned to make him see differently.

"He comes every Wednesday, Friday, and Sunday." She rolled her eyes and then grinned. "He brings my favorite flowers, and we have lunch or dinner. Sometimes we go to the movies if there's something good playing."

"I'm sure you enjoy that."

She sat down on the bed and pressed her hands palm side down into the mattress.

"I'm ready to come home," she blurted, smiling up at me. "But your dad... He's skeptical."

"Well," I started, leaning my back against the wall. "His feelings are valid, ma. You've been home a few times, and each lasted a few months before you..."

I let my voice trail off, but she knew where I was going with my statement. When my mother had her first breakdown, she'd been kept in the hospital for weeks before the doctors let her come home. Two months later, she broke again, and it was worse than before. That time around, she spent six months in a psychiatric hospital. She'd gone through intensive therapy, and they thought after her treatment that she could function with the help of her family and continuous therapy. Well, she came home, and she was good for years, then two years ago, shit hit the fan, and my father couldn't handle it anymore.

"I know my head will never be better, but I want to work at it. My parents...they fucked me up, Lenny. I hope I didn't do the same to you and your brother."

I shook my head and said, "Nah, we turned out pretty great."

"On the outside," she murmured. "But what about inside, Lenny? How do you feel in there?" She pointed to her head and then mine.

I moved from my spot against the wall and sat down next to her on the bed.

"Do you remember telling Nard and me during our visits

with you to always protect our mental health? Your exact words were to—"

"Never let society's view of Black men when it comes to their mental health stop you from getting help if you need it," she finished, nodding. "Glad to know you two were listening."

"We always listened, even when we shouldn't have been." I grabbed her hand with both of mine and stared into the dark eyes that mirrored my own. "Invite dad to therapy with you, and we'll go from there."

She'd been reluctant to let him in on her therapy sessions, but allowing him to do so would make all the difference. It would be a step in the right direction, that I was sure of.

"I-I can do that."

That was all I needed to hear.

A couple of hours later, I was sitting in my father's home with my brother, his wife, and their tribe of kids. This was the first weekend I'd been home in about two months, and the old man wanted to have a family dinner before I headed back to Philly. This also gave me the opportunity to talk to him about changing up some things.

"So, what do you think he'll say?" I asked Nard. My brother gave me a knowing look, and I sighed.

"I know what mom said yesterday, but she's been home before, and you see how that turned out."

"I know, but—"

"You always had more faith in her than me," he said, cutting me off. "Sometimes I look at Tamera, and I think 'what if she goes through something traumatic' and then I have to—"

"That won't happen, she's strong."

"Mom is strong too." He chuckled. "It seems weird saying that, but she is."

I nodded, understanding what he meant. There was this notion that people with mental health issues weren't strong or couldn't handle things like another person would. Our mother had endured a lot, and she'd been able to keep herself in check for a long time. That showed her strength and willfulness. But I had always been a believer in the past eventually mixing with your present if it's not handled properly. Our mother was the perfect example of that.

"Well—"

"Uncle Lenny, look at what my grandpa got me," Kendall yelled, running into the room with her baby sister in tow. I picked up my favorite girl Kaylie and pulled on her ponytails. Kendall showed us the Barbie she was gifted and explained why she was happy that it was Black.

"Uncle Wenny, I-I want a Barbie," Kaylie pleaded with wide eyes. "Can I have one?"

"Sure, baby girl, I'll get you a Barbie."

"But one that's different than mine, so we don't get them mixed up," Kendall suggested, holding the doll closer to my face.

Laughing, Nard said, "We'll make sure it's not the same, kid."

"Thanks, daddy," she chirped before taking off. Kaylie wiggled out of my lap and took off after her sister. I glanced at my brother with a grin on my face, and he shook his head.

"Don't even say it," he started. "I hope I get another boy." Leonard and Tamera had three boys and two girls. "At least we'll outnumber them by two."

"I'm sure that'll help."

He snorted, letting me know he knew that it wouldn't matter. Those girls of his had him wrapped around their little fingers.

"Should we go talk to dad before dinner is ready?" I took a deep breath and stood.

"Let's do it."

As we entered the kitchen, our father looked up from the magazine he was flipping through. He and Leonard looked just alike while I favored our mother more. He moved his light brown eyes between the two of us and then began to shake his head.

"Whatever it is that you two are up to, I don't want any parts."

"Pop, you didn't even give us a chance to—"

"The answer is still no." He gave us one of those looks we got when we were kids and up to no good. I couldn't help the smile that spread across my face, and when I looked over at my brother, he had the same smile plastered on his.

"It's about mom," I reasoned, removing the smile from my face. His eyes softened, and he nodded for us to sit down.

"What is it?"

I glanced at Nard as he said, "We think it's time to bring her home."

The look on my father's face told me that he'd been thinking the same thing all along.

SEVEN

MAGNOLIA

"Okay, Aunt Lori, I'm positive that your fried chicken definitely has crack in it," Juniper said before biting into another piece. Our aunt rolled her eyes as she always did when we commented on how good her chicken was.

"All I know is that this baby of mine is loving this grease," Nova groaned, licking her lips. "I can't drink, but I can definitely eat this chicken."

"I made extra just for you," Lori said, pulling hot chicken out of the deep fryer.

"Hold up," I said, eyeing my aunt as she dumped the golden wings into a bowl lined with paper towel. "Just for her?"

"Yup, she's eating for two!"

"But that's not fair," Brynlee whined. "I don't get to eat like this often, what about me?" Brynlee was a professional ballerina, and they had strict diets. She tried her best to follow it, but sometimes she slipped up. The one good thing about her body was that no matter how much she ate, she never seemed to gain weight.

"I just want some more," I said, smiling. Lori looked between the eight of us and shook her head. The rest of the girls weren't saying anything, but she knew they were thinking just as we were.

"Fine, I'll cook the rest of it, but that means you're on your own for breakfast."

"I have breakfast under control," Lilac offered. The conversation in the kitchen changed quickly when Lori asked Elena about how she and Noah were doing.

"We're doing pretty great," she answered, shrugging. Nova stopped mid-chew and eyed her curiously.

"What did he do?" she asked. "And don't tell me nothing, I can tell by the way you answered that something is wrong."

Nova and Noah were twins. She knew him better than anyone.

"He didn't do anything bad... He just wants us to move in together, and I don't think I'm ready."

"Why not?" I asked. Their relationship was still fresh, but Noah and Elena had a different type of bond. Anyone who got to experience it up close could see it. They were meant to be.

"Well... I just got my own space after living and taking care of my mom for so many years. Then I moved to New York and lived with Elijah until he moved out. I like the space."

"And Noah feels a way?"

"Not necessarily. He was actually okay with my reasoning."

"Oh, I get it," Blossom chimed in. "You wanted him to be mad or push for it a little more."

"Does that sound crazy?"

"It sounds like you want to move in with him. You probably already stay there more than you do your own place," Lori said, placing her hands on the counter. "What we won't do, ladies, is cause more drama in our lives because we aren't communicating what we want and how we want it."

I smiled at Lori.

She was so dope and always had been. She made you feel comfortable to the point where you'd open up about anything without feeling like you'd be judged. It made me wonder how my father and her were related.

"You're right," Elena agreed, standing from her seat. "I'm going to call him. I'll be back." As if on cue, my phone began to vibrate on the counter. I glanced down at it and tried to hide my smile. Lennox and I had been texting back and forth since he left on Friday for Jersey. Our conversation ranged from serious to pure comedy. I looked forward to it all. I opened his text and frowned.

> You never answered my question.

> What question?

> How will your life change after this weekend?

Ah. That one.

The one that I had purposely ignored. It wasn't that I didn't want to discuss how things would change for me after I met with my father. I wanted to break it all down to him, but doing so would leave me vulnerable. It was tough for me to allow that. Deep down, I wanted to bare my soul to Lennox, but the thought of doing so terrified me.

> Can I explain another day?

He replied a few minutes later with:

> Whenever you're ready, Lia.

"Anybody want any more wine?" I asked, standing to grab the chilled bottle from the freezer. After pouring more for who wanted some, I took a long sip from my glass. "I got jealous when Lennox told me about his ex-wife visiting him at work." All eyes landed on me, and I took another sip. Elena walked back into the kitchen just as the conversation started up. "Why would I get jealous? We aren't in a relationship. We aren't having sex. I mean, I barely know him."

"But you like him," Blossom said.

"I really, really like him," I admitted. "So much, and I'm scared."

"Scared that—"

"That what dad did to us, the person I ultimately fall in love with will do it to me," I cut in, finishing Lilac's statement. Her eyes filled with tears, and I was done for after that. Admitting it out loud felt good, but it didn't stop me from feeling sad that this was my reality. "Why didn't that bastard step up? Huh?"

"Because he's a fuck nigga!" Juniper spat. "And he doesn't get to make you...make *us* feel that way!"

"More than that," Blossom said. "I barely remember him. How crazy is that?"

The room became eerily silent, and I forced my eyes closed while wiping the free-falling tears from my face. When a pair of arms wrapped around me, I took a deep breath and opened my eyes.

It was Elena.

"It's okay to feel how you guys feel," she murmured, stepping back. She glanced around the room and then added, "Sometimes you have to face things head-on." Elena knew better than anyone what it felt like to have an absent father. Her situation was a lot different than ours, but she'd still experienced life without her dad, and it sucked.

"So you think we should find him and...and what?"

"Talk to him," Lori answered.

"He doesn't deserve that," Lilac chimed in. "He doesn't deserve to know any of us as we are now. We are what we are because of mama and Lori." She shook her head.

"It's not so he can get to know you," Lori continued. "It's so you girls can let go of this hurt you've been harboring."

It was times like this that I didn't understand Lori's stance.

She didn't speak to any of her family. Growing up, she didn't talk about them, and they weren't a part of our lives. I'd always wondered how they felt about her taking us in. I wondered on many nights how Gerald—our father—felt about it. Him giving up his rights should have been answer enough, but it wasn't.

"And what hurt have you been harboring, Auntie?" Daisy asked, tilting her head sideways. "You left Philly before Mags was even born, and you hate coming back. We have to beg you to come visit us."

Leave it to her to ask what we've all been thinking. I hated that this was the turn our girls' weekend had taken, but here we were. I'd have to make it up to the girls another time.

Lori looked horrified by the question. It was the first time I'd ever seen that look on her face.

"I let my hurt go a long time ago, and it isn't relevant to your situation." She stormed out of the kitchen, leaving us all stunned.

What the hell just happened?

"That didn't go well," Nova murmured, rubbing her belly. "I think she needs time."

"I didn't ask the question to upset her." Daisy sighed and stood from her chair. "I need a nap." She left the kitchen, and soon after, everyone began to disperse. Our night had been ruined, and there was nothing I could do about it, so I retreated to my bedroom and did the one thing that I knew would make me feel somewhat better.

"WHAT'S WRONG, LIA?" Lennox asked.

I wiped tears from my face and held the phone tighter to my ear.

"I just... I'm not happy right now." I'd called him because I needed someone to talk to, but we'd been on the phone for an hour now, and I still hadn't opened up.

"That's what you've been saying since we got on the phone. So how about we talk about something else until you feel comfortable?"

"Well, my aunt fried chicken today, and I swear we would all fight over it if she hadn't made more." His raspy laugh filled my ears, and the heaviness in my heart begin to lift.

"I need to try some of it if it's causing fights."

"I'm sure she wouldn't mind making you some."

"You told her about me?"

"I told her that I had this guy friend who's pretty dope."

He was more than dope, though. I'd told her that too.

"Pretty dope," he repeated, chuckling. "I like the sound of that."

"Lennox, can you tell me something about you that I don't know?"

"The things that you don't know about me are intense, Lia." His response only made me want to know. "Are you sure you want to open that door?"

"What door would I be opening?"

"The one where if I tell you about this part of my life, then you have to open up to me about the part of yours that keeps you so closed off."

"I want to know," I whispered, swallowing back the urge to renege.

He took a deep breath and then said, "I guess I can start with my mother."

By the time he'd finished telling me about his mother, I was damn near in tears. She'd endured so much as a young girl, and it festered until she couldn't take any more. She broke, and I didn't want that for myself. I felt her pain. I hadn't been physically abused like she had, but mentally... Mentally, I'd been through a lot. To not be wanted by the one man that was supposed to love me before any other is so fucked up.

"I'm sorry about your mom."

"There's nothing to be sorry for, she's a trooper."

"Do you think your dad will give in and bring her home?"

"Yeah, he misses having her around, but I'm not sure how well it will work."

"I think it'll work."

"Yeah?"

"Mmm, it has to."

"You sound invested, beautiful." Lennox had been hitting me with subtle compliments all night. I had a feeling that he wasn't doing it knowingly, and honestly, I loved it. I loved how he was so sweet without even trying.

"I mean, you're basically my best friend now, so yes, I am definitely invested," I finally said.

"Do you know the first rule of two people being best friends?"

"No secrets," I murmured, turning in bed. "You want to know about me."

"I want to know everything, Lia."

"Because we're friends." The word *friend* felt sour in my mouth, and I didn't like it. I knew that it was up to me to change the dynamic between us. "Friends that tell each other everything."

"You can talk to me."

"I... When I was fifteen, my mother died from lupus complications."

"I'm sorry, Lia. I had no idea. We don't—"

"I know... It's just in order for you to understand the rest, you needed to hear that first." I let the silence that settled between us linger for a few minutes before continuing. "So...my dad left when I was nine, and my mother raised us so well. We were happy, you know? And then we weren't."

"Is your father alive?"

"He's alive, but he might as well be dead. When my mother passed, social services reached out to him, and he answered by signing his rights away and leaving us in the custody of the state. He abandoned us not once but twice, Lennox. And now I'm damaged. I can't even let someone get close to me without freaking out."

"Lia," he started, sighing. "I apologize for what your father did to you." His words sparked tears.

"You don't—"

"No, I do have to apologize for him because sometimes you need to hear the words, even if they aren't coming from the person who should be saying them. I apologize that he left you. I'm sorry he made you feel like you weren't good enough for his love, but Lia, baby, you are good enough for that four-letter word. You're good enough for the love I want to give you, and you deserve the love of the people around you."

"When are you coming home?" I asked, wiping my eyes and face clean. "I want to thank you in person."

"Thank me for what?"

"For making me realize something that I'd rather talk about face to face."

"Sunday afternoon."

"Can I see you?"

"Afternoon or night?" he asked.

"Well...maybe both," I answered. "If that's alright with you."

"It's more than alright."

It was then that our fate was sealed. Whether Lennox knew it or not at the moment didn't matter. He would know by the end of Sunday night. I would make sure of that.

"Are you sleeping, Mags?" Daisy whispered from the door.

"No," I said, turning to face her. Lennox and I had hung up a little while ago, and I'd been laying here staring into space. Lori's reaction to Daisy's question weighed heavily on my mind.

"Can we come in?" She pulled the door open further, showing me the rest of my clan of sisters behind her. I nodded, and they accosted me in seconds. Blossom was the last to climb into my king-sized bed with us, but she made sure to get a spot close to me. My big baby.

"Why are you guys still awake?"

"Couldn't sleep," Lilac answered. "All of us."

"Yeah, me either." I sighed. "Lori on y'all mind too?" I got a series of nods, and it became clear that we all got the same vibe from Lori.

"What do you think happened?" Juniper asked. "It can't have anything to do with dad because she's pushing for us to meet him."

"Doesn't matter," Blossom sassed, slicing a hand through the air. "He's still a fuck nigga, and he doesn't deserve us, no matter what's up with Lori."

Blossom's words were enough to silence us all. I could feel their heavy thoughts, and it was weighing on me. So instead of letting this shit show of a weekend fall even more, I decided to lighten the mood.

"I'm going to have sex with Lennox on Sunday." A round of gasps filled the air, and I laughed. "He's just so damn—"

"Handsome," Blossom finished in a lighthearted voice. "He has these really dark eyes that kind of slant when he laughs, and they match his freaking skin. He's also tall. Really tall."

"How is it that Blossom has met him, but the rest of us haven't?" Daisy asked, sitting up and crossing her legs. "I mean, it should have gone in order from oldest to youngest."

"And why is that, Dais?" Lilac gave her a hard stare, and I rolled my eyes. She was just being difficult because that's what she does.

Before they could get going, I said, "Let's not start a debate. I just told you guys I'm going to have sex with him, and you want to argue about who met him first?"

"Girl, please," Blossom said, waving me off. "It's about time you spread those pretty chocolate legs and get off."

"Amen to that," the others agreed, laughing.

"It's been two years since I've..."

"We know!" they exclaimed in unison.

"I need pointers!"

I didn't need them, but I was guilty of egging on their shenanigans at times. This would be one of them.

Juniper jumped off the bed and laid on the floor. She lifted her legs up into the air and spread them.

"Okay," she started. "So, this position is my favorite because I feel everything."

"Ew, that one is not it," I said, shaking my head.

"I think having your legs pinned back behind your head is the way to go," Daisy mused, grinning.

"Ass up, face down for me," Lilac added on. I glanced at each one of them mimicking their favorite sex position and fell out laughing.

"You guys are sick, but I'll take these into consideration."

"Come on, Mags, what does it for you?" Juniper asked, repositioning her body so that she was sitting Indian-style. "What really gets you off?"

"I prefer being on top," I replied, shrugging. "That way if—"

"He can't get you off, then you can get yourself off," they finished for me. Our laughter filled the room, and it was an amazing feeling. This was so much better than how the night had ended.

EIGHT

LENNOX

SUNDAY NIGHT...

I sat in my truck outside of Magnolia's townhome, waiting for her to emerge. She insisted that I wait for her instead of ringing the doorbell like I was itching to do. I glanced at my watch again and frowned. It had been thirty minutes since I pulled up, and she had me impatiently waiting.

A few more minutes passed before I decided to turn the truck off and get out. I glanced around her quiet neighborhood and then ascended the steps to her door. I raised my hand to knock, but the connection to the wood never happened.

There she was...

Standing in front of me in a lace bra and panty set with thigh-high boots. I couldn't stop looking her over. Her body was a work of art. Magnolia was just my type, thick in all the right places and confident about it. I opened and closed my mouth, trying to will the words out, but nothing.

"I was wondering when you'd get tired of waiting," she said, chuckling.

"It was on purpose," I managed to say. She smiled broadly, showing off her pretty teeth, and then stepped back to allow me inside. I took my time passing her, moving my eyes from her feet to her makeup-free face.

Gorgeous was an understatement.

"I think—"

The door shut, and I was on her before she could finish the statement.

"Let's not think," I whispered, pushing her into the door. Her chest heaved, but her breathing was steady. I eyed her once more, taking in the package that I'd soon be unwrapping. "I need you to know...whatever you were about to say, I need you to know that it's what you want."

"I want you," she said, licking her lips. "I know that I want you to fuck me."

"You *need* me to fuck you," I repeated, moving toward her with purpose. She nodded in response, but I wasn't asking. I just wanted to know what the words tasted like on my tongue. What I really wanted to know was what *she* tasted like on my tongue.

Not wanting to waste any more time, I reached for Magnolia and lifted her into my arms. She squealed but didn't hesitate to wrap her toned legs around my waist and her arms around my neck. "Where's your bedroom?" I was moving toward the staircase in long strides.

"Upstairs, last door to the left."

I guided us carefully up the spiral staircase while getting my fill of her luscious ass. I'm a man—a respectful one—but a man, nonetheless. I'd noticed all the ass she carried around, and I'd be a fool not to take advantage of this moment. I didn't know this would be her way of thanking me, but I wasn't complaining. If anything, I was rejoicing. She had no idea how bad I've wanted this. How bad I've wanted her like *this*. Since the moment I laid eyes on her beautiful ass, I'd craved her. I was good at suppressing, but she just let out a monster.

"I can feel how hard you are." Her words brought me back to the present. I let my inner thoughts simmer and focused my attention on the task at hand: getting us to her bedroom.

"That happens when you answer the door damn near naked and looking as good as you do."

I pushed my way into her bedroom and stopped in front of the bed. I dropped Magnolia onto the mattress and climbed between her legs. Her eyes... They were watching my every move. Studying me.

"Thank you," she whispered, then bit down on her lip.

"Why am I being thanked?" I asked, running my fingers along her neckline. Her skin was as soft as I thought it would be.

"For being a man who knows what's right and what's not," she murmured, slipping a hand underneath my shirt. Her fingers moved along my abs, and she smiled. "I always knew you were built nice. You should take this off."

She pulled at the fabric, and I reluctantly removed my hands from her so that I could dispose of the barrier between us. While I was at it, I stood to get rid of my shoes and jeans, leaving me in my boxer briefs. I looked down and shook my head at my erection. It was hard as a brick, and the tip of my dick was poking through the elastic band.

"I can take care of that for you."

"Not until I take care of you first," I said, lifting my eyes to meet her heated gaze. The shit was intoxicating. I hadn't had an ounce of liquor, but I felt like I was drunk. That feeling of something strong burning your throat and warming your chest before settling in your stomach was prominent right now. "But before I do anything to that beautiful ass body of yours, tell me something, Lia." I retook my position between her legs and reached for the straps on her bra.

"Anything," she gasped, eyes widening at my invasion of her plump breasts. After halfway removing the lacy fabric, I rolled both of her hard chocolate nipples between my thumb and index finger. I was satisfied with the low whimpers leaving her lips. My touch caused that.

"If I give you this dick, are you still going to hold back?" I asked, leaning forward to run my lips lightly against her cheek. I wanted to kiss her, to feel how soft her thick lips were, but I settled near her ear and added, "Or will you let me in, baby?"

"I want to let you in."

I shook my head and buried it into her neck. She smelled like something floral, and I inhaled deeper so that the scent would be embedded for a lifetime.

"I *need* you to let me in," I countered, lifting my head so that I could see her face and she could see mine. She needed to know how genuine I was about this. "Completely. Can you do that?" I inched forward, letting my lips linger lightly against hers.

"Y-yes," she answered, closing the space.

There were immediate fireworks at the connection. Her nipples scraped against my chest as we kissed. Magnolia parted her mouth and let out a moan. I took advantage of the space by slipping my tongue inside and tangling it with hers. I took control, and she didn't fight it; instead, she submitted to my power, and it turned me the fuck on. "Please."

I broke our kiss and hovered over her. I couldn't stare too long. The plea in her hooded gaze was one I couldn't take. I wanted to be selfish for a while. I wanted to explore her body just as I had imagined many times before. How could I do that if she was staring at me like that? Begging me with those beautiful irises to fuck her senseless.

Shaking my head, I said, "You're dangerous."

"Please," she murmured, slipping her soft hand into my boxers and then wrapping it around my dick. I lost all resolve.

"Fuck it." I hooked my fingers into her thong and began to slip it from her body. My eyes locked onto her waxed mound as it came into view, and I licked my lips. My mouth was watering at the sight. After tossing the thong aside and removing my boxers, I lifted one of her legs onto my shoulder and pushed the other to the side. Her slick lips parted, and I zeroed in on her pearl. "Touch yourself."

I took pleasure in watching her hand slowly move past her breasts, down her toned stomach, and then landing right where I wanted. Magnolia wasted no time going for her clit, but I stopped her.

"No, slip two fingers in," I said, using my free hand to guide her. "I want to show you something." Two manicured fingers disappeared inside of her, and I smiled.

"W-what next?" she gasped, eyes rolling back. I'd told her to do it, but I couldn't help assisting. As I used her fingers to pleasure her, I leaned myself forward with her leg still propped on my shoulder. With her body angled just how I needed, I replaced her fingers with mine. Her eyes fluttered, and then the moans commenced. "That's my—"

"It's your spot," I finished for her. "I know. Does it feel good, baby?"

"W-what are you doing to me?"

I chuckled at the question but didn't answer. She would know soon enough that I had her right where I wanted her.

"Rub your clit, Lia," I ordered, picking up speed. I pushed my fingers in and out, and every time I pressed into her g-spot, she tightened her pussy muscles around them. Her reaction... I'd never get tired of seeing how my touch made her react. She was more responsive than any woman I've ever been with, and I was enjoying it. Maybe a little too much. "You don't even know how beautiful you look like this."

"Len-nox... I'm—" As her body seized, I removed my fingers, let go of her leg, and dived in face first. "Ooooh, God."

I moved my tongue skillfully over her clit. Her pleas for me to stop didn't go unnoticed. I got my fill and then gave her what she wanted. I watched her come down from the orgasm while licking her essence from my mouth and fingers. She was my new favorite dessert.

"How do you feel?" I asked, chuckling at her eyes opening and closing. She was on the verge of sleep.

"Like... I don't even have words to explain what you just did to me," she answered. She'd managed to focus her attention on me, and the look of satisfaction in her gaze was enough for me to call this a win. I wanted to have sex with Magnolia. Scratch that, I wanted to fuck the shit out of her while giving her orgasm after orgasm. But what I didn't want was for it to happen like this. A thank you? Nah. I didn't need sex as a thank you for being a man.

"Lennox... Why do I get the feeling that's the only thing happening tonight?"

"Because it is." Her eyes were on my erection, and I was tempted. Lord knows I was tempted to ask her to help me with it, but it didn't feel right. I removed myself from between her legs and grabbed my boxers. As I slipped them on, she sat up in bed with a confused expression on her face.

"Did I do something?"

I couldn't stop the laugh that slipped.

"The only thing you did was look sexy as hell while reaching that high." She smirked, but the confusion was still there. I stood in front of the bed and began to remove her boots. "You did nothing wrong, Lia."

"Then what is it?"

I tossed the first boot and then worked on the next. Once I had the second one off, I reached for my shirt and then handed it to her. I climbed into bed next to her and said, "I don't need sex as a thank you." She slipped my shirt on and pulled it down onto her body.

"I didn't mean it that way," she said, laying her body next to mine. "I guess I just..."

"You just what?" She looked embarrassed, and that wasn't my goal here. She closed her eyes and dropped her head. I lightly gripped her chin and tilted her head up. "Let me see them."

"No, because then you'll see that they're watery."

"I made you want to cry?"

"No."

I leaned forward and kissed her lips. I repeated the action a few times and then kissed both eyelids. A little smile formed on her lips, and my heartbeats calmed.

"Let me see."

"You know," she started, giving me what I wanted, "most men

would jump at the chance to fuck me." Her eyes held an amused glint, but I also knew she was serious. She felt like I'd rejected her, and that was the furthest thing from the truth.

"Let's get something straight." I began to run my fingers along her jawline. With her hair pulled up into a tight bun, I got the perfect view of her features. She was a work of art, every inch of her. "I'm not most men. Sex is not a bargaining chip, it isn't a reward for good behavior, and it doesn't solve problems. So, while I would love to work the fuck out of you, I can't. Not like this."

"I— Why are you like this?"

Laughing, I said, "Enlighten me."

"You just... You say things that make me feel good, but they also make me think."

"What I just said made you feel good?"

She nodded. "It proves that only being friends with you won't work for me."

"Yeah?"

She confirmed her statement with another nod, and I leaned in for a kiss. Her lips were hard to stay away from. They complimented mine well. I pulled her body close and she yelped.

"Jesus, Lennox," she said, grinning up at me. "Are you sure you don't want me to take care of that? Because I do this really cool thing with my tongue and—"

"Yo," I cut in, laughing. "Chill. We'll get there."

She shrugged and said, "Suit yourself. I got mine."

"Now you want to be a comedian?"

"I did win class clown in high school. I can tell pretty good jokes." I eyed her skeptically, and she smiled broadly. "Knock, knock."

I shook my head. "Nah. We aren't doing knock-knock jokes."

"Come on," she begged, sitting up. "Knock, knock." All it took was her poking her lip out for me to give in.

"Who's there?"

"This."

"This who?" I knew where she was going with it, and I was already laughing. A mischievous look flashed in her eyes, but it was gone too soon for me to address. She batted her eyes at me and leaned forward.

Licking her lips, she said, "This dick," and reached for mine. "Let me taste it."

"That's the joke?" Her fingers moved slowly over the length of my dick. Even through my boxers, it felt amazing. I could only imagine what her mouth would feel like.

"It's the best I could come up with."

"I-I find that hard to believe," I murmured. Not being able to take the lack of contact anymore, I took her hand and held onto it while I pushed my boxers down. She was on me before I could blink. Her warm tongue moved from base to tip several times.

"You're blessed," she whispered into the tip of my dick before swallowing me whole.

"F-fuck."

"Mmmm..."

I was a goner the second her tongue wrapped around me, and she used it along with her mouth to suck me dry. I was marrying her one day. She'd just sealed the deal with that move and didn't even know it.

NINE

MAGNOLIA

"You've been in that corner reading for an hour," Lennox complained from his spot in my bed. He passed out right after I finished giving him what I'm sure was the best head of his life—his words, not mine. I looked up from my book and gave him an annoyed look, though I was anything but.

"You slept for like three hours, and you don't see me complaining."

"And that's my fault?" he asked, lifting his eyebrows suggestively. "That mouth is dangerous." I rolled my eyes and then glanced down to hide my smile. I focused my attention back on my read for the month. It was a mystery with a splash of romance by an author named Parker Vincent.

"What are you reading anyway?" he asked, snatching the book from my hands.

"Hey!" He scanned the front, and the playful smile that was once on his face disappeared. He glanced at me and then back at the book. "What?"

"Nothing," he answered, handing it back to me. "What is it about?" He was deflecting, but I played along.

"Well... it follows this young man who doesn't understand what's happening in his life or why."

"Tell me more." He'd taken up a spot next to me on the padded window bench I had inside of my room. It was my favorite spot to lounge in.

"In the first few pages, he speaks about feeling cursed and how his life is like a revolving door of bad things happening."

"Mmm," he hummed.

"I also think this is more of a romance than a mystery." His lips twitched, but he nodded for me to go on. "Okay, so the hero is dating this girl he met at a college party, and for me, the story draws me in more when they're together. The author, she's really good with words. I know most writers consider themselves poets, but she's on another level. I'm sucked in by every word written."

"What makes you think the author is a woman?"

I shrugged. "I just guessed because of the name, and there isn't a picture inside to tell me otherwise."

"That's the first book by that author, do you have the second one?"

I grabbed the book he was speaking of from the shelf beside me and handed it to him.

"How did you know that? Have you read these before?" I wouldn't be surprised if he had. Lennox loved to read, and it was one of the things we bonded over when we first began to talk.

"Something like that," he murmured, flipping through the book.

"I kind of read them out of order, so I'm pretty sure the hero and heroine got married eventually and then broke up."

"What makes you think that?"

"Well, in that book, the hero seems to be working through his inner demons. It never mentions a divorce, but the heroine from book one is never mentioned either. I'm putting two and two together."

"Your view on these... No one has ever guessed that it's more romance than anything." He was staring at me in awe. "I knew you were special, man."

"I feel as if I'm not following."

"I wrote them," he said, taking the paperback from my hand. He slipped a bookmark between the pages and then set the book on top of the other. "I wrote them."

"Y-you..." I shook my head. "Lennox, what?"

"I write under an alias because I didn't want the attention if they were to blow up."

"You're Parker Vincent?" He nodded. "A New York Times bestselling author?" I pointed to the label on the book to be sure he understood what I was asking him.

"Yeah, that too."

"What the... I'm— I don't have words." I glanced down at the books sitting between us. This was a surreal moment. Lennox was so much more than I'd ever thought. He was fucking amazing.

"Are you mad?"

I snapped my head in his direction. "Mad? Why would I be mad?"

"Because I didn't tell you before now."

"That's crazy." I waved him off. "I invited you to a store me and my sisters own without telling you that we owned one first. I think we can call it even."

If anyone understood his stance on not wanting to be in the limelight, it was me. My sisters and I liked being low key. We brought in a lot of business, and though we could take the store global, it wasn't a goal of ours. We were blessed to be able to profit big off the city, and we were content with that.

"You said I was the first person to ever guess that it's a romance."

"Yeah, everyone gets wrapped up in the action that they don't see the truth right there in my words."

"I— You're an amazing writer, Lennox," I complimented, moving the books from between us so that I could scoot closer. "The way you convey both stories is beautiful. Now that I know you wrote them, I'm going to take a guess and say that you were telling your own story in so many words."

"It's an accurate guess. I wrote them both after the divorce. I had a lot I needed to get off my chest, and I was able to do that in the form of two books."

"Is the curse you believe your hero has a way of talking about your mother's mental illness without disrespecting her?"

"It is."

I wrapped my arms around his torso and laid my head on his shoulder.

"Thank you for telling me."

"I couldn't keep it from you even if I tried. Not after seeing you read it." We sat in comfortable silence, and through it, I felt us becoming closer. I was wrong before. This moment right here, right now was the shift in our dynamic. There was no going back now.

"SO HE ATE that pussy up and is making you wait for the dick?" Lilac asked, laughing. I glared at her, but it didn't last long. Soon, I was laughing right along with her. "That is a *man*."

"Such a man," I agreed, smiling. Lennox and I had spent our entire Sunday chilling around my townhome, talking about everything under the sun. I learned so much about him, and it only added to my reasons why I was so into him. Now I was spilling the tea to my sisters not even twenty-four hours later.

"Let's not forget she sucked that man's dick after telling a knock-knock joke," Juniper pointed out.

"Freaky ass hoe," Blossom blurted. "I thought you were out of practice."

"Shit, me too. I guess I still got it because my little tongue trick knocked his ass right out." I'd chosen to keep him being an author—a successful one—to myself. It wasn't my place to reveal his secret, and I wouldn't.

"I've been trying to master that for years," Daisy murmured, shaking her head. "I just can't get the motion right."

"You have to wrap, then suck, sis," Blossom coached, using two fingers. "Like this." I shook my head at them as they demonstrated how it should be done. Turning toward the stove, I got started on our meal for the night.

Lilac came to stand next to me while I dropped the onions, garlic, and green peppers I'd diced into a pan coated with two sticks of butter.

"Do you want to reach out to dad?" she whispered. I nodded.

"I need to," I said. "You guys don't have to if you don't want, but I need to do this for me and my state of mind."

"I understand." She bumped my shoulder. "I'll do it with you."

"Me too," Juniper added from behind us. "We can hear you."

"I will, too," Daisy said. I turned to face them, and my eyes landed on Blossom immediately. She was fumbling with her fingers and pouting.

"It's okay if you aren't ready, Bloss."

"I can't do it," she whispered. "I barely remember him, and I just... I'm not ready." She gave us each a watery smile and then added, "But I'll be around for you guys afterward."

"We know," Daisy assured her. I had a feeling that it would take Blossom longer to come to terms with what was happening. She wasn't as affected because he left before the memories of him settled into her mind. The effects of not having a male figure were still weighing on her shoulders, that much I knew. Eventually, she'd realize that she needed this as much as the rest of us, and we'd be here to see her through it.

"When will dinner be ready?" Juniper asked, changing subjects. The tension in the room dissipated immediately.

"When I'm finished," I said, smacking her hand away from the stove. "Go find something to do with yourself. All of you."

"You're not mom," they said simultaneously.

"It's either that or I send y'all home hungry." Bodies began to move, and I smiled. That was easy.

"Oh, Mags?" Juniper called out, stopping in front of the fridge.

"Mmm."

"Can you cover my day at the store this week?" I cut an eye at her and then glanced back at the stove.

"Is there a legit reason why you can't do it?"

"Brandon reached out to me." That got my attention. I covered the chicken thighs and turned to face her.

"Brandon, as in Brynlee's younger brother." She nodded.

"Yeah, apparently he lives here now, and he wants to catch up."

"Are you sure you want to go there again?" Brandon was a pretty great dude, and his sister was obviously one of our closest friends, but he and Juniper had weird history. He never caught on to her feelings for him, or he simply ignored the signs. She was heartbroken, but she got over it. I couldn't see her hurt like that again.

"It's not like that," she said, waving a hand in the air. "We're just catching up. So, can you cover me?"

"Yeah, I got you." She smiled and skipped off to the living room. Once she was out of view, I grabbed my phone to call Brynlee.

"Hey girl, hey," she chirped after picking up.

"You did not tell me that Brandon lives here now."

"Oh god," she groaned. "Did he reach out to Juniper yet? Never mind because if you're calling, then he has."

"They're hanging out this week. What's his deal?"

"I wish I knew the answer to that, Mags." She huffed and then added, "He was acting weird when I brought Juni up. I always thought he only saw her as a friend, but I'm starting to think there's another reason why he didn't pursue her."

"Do you think he's going to try now?"

"I think he's in a different headspace, and I also know he chose Philly because of her."

"Mmm, interesting."

"Very," she murmured. We talked a little longer and then said our goodbyes. I set my phone down and frowned. I guess there wasn't a shift going on in just my life. There was something serious happening in the universe, and it was about to hit us all.

Hard.

Later that night, after my sisters were long gone, I was startled by a loud knocking on my front door. I set my glass of wine and book down and then walked toward the door. I took a peek out of the peephole, then quickly pulled it open after seeing who it was.

"Lennox," I spoke, running my gaze down the length of his tall frame. As my eyes found his again, he gave me a charming smile and then held up a book. "What's that?" I stepped back to allow him inside.

"You said you wanted to know what Toni Morrison book my students picked, and this is it," he responded, handing it over to me.

"*A Mercy*," I said, after glancing at the cover. I hadn't had the pleasure of reading this particular title by the late Toni Morrison, but I knew what it was about. "They actually picked this one?" I had planned on grabbing a copy of each novel I'd never read of hers. It was my way of paying homage to her greatness.

"I was a little surprised myself, but yes." I had no time to reply because he was on me within seconds. His strong arms pulled me into his solid body, and then those juicy lips were on mine completely, taking my breath away. The lips on this man were crafted by God himself. He took his sweet time, making them perfect for me and me alone.

"Is this why you came here?" I muttered into his mouth. "To kiss me?"

"Guilty." We kissed some more, taking our time exploring the depths of each other's mouths as if we hadn't had the pleasure of doing so before, and then he pulled back. "And now I have to go."

"Aw, man, but you just got here." I poked my lip out, and he chuckled.

He leaned in to kiss my forehead and then said, "I didn't think this through when the idea to pop up came to me, but I really do have to go. I've been slacking on grading papers."

"Well, I guess I'll let you go." I walked him to the door and stepped out as he swaggered down the steps. He glanced over his shoulder at me and smirked. Once he was in his truck and then off my block, I retreated into my townhome and shut the door. I was certain that the smile on my face would be hard to knock off, and it was all because of Lennox. He was something special, and my heart wanted him around forever.

TEN

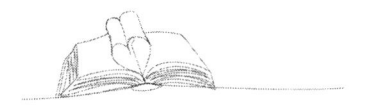

LENNOX

"What did he say again?"

I talked to my brother over the car stereo while trying to figure out what was going on in Magnolia's mind at the moment. She'd been quiet since leaving the restaurant we dined at tonight, and I was a little worried. During dinner, she kept a smile on her face, and giggles stayed slipping from her mouth, but then she got a text, and that changed. It was as if someone sucked the personality right out of her, and I wasn't feeling it. I wanted to get to the bottom of her sudden mood change, but she insisted that I take my brother's call, so I obliged.

"Therapy went good today, and he sees progress," my brother replied after yelling at his daughter to stop knocking on his co-worker's office doors.

I chuckled.

He only brought her to work with him when she was "sick." Kendall was great at playing sick. Leonard worked long nights sometimes, so it didn't surprise me that he was still in the office at nine o'clock at night.

"But..." The sigh that settled in the air told me all I needed to know. "He still isn't ready."

"He's ready, but he's hesitant."

I grabbed Magnolia's hand to stop her from fidgeting.

"Thanks for the update, Nard," I said. "But let me call you back." I hung up and grabbed her other hand.

"Dinner was good, right?"

"Yes," she whispered, giving me an almost sultry look. "I'm just nervous about calling my dad."

Ah.

She'd told me about wanting to reach out to him.

"How about you call him right now while I'm here with you?" I suggested. "Your aunt sent his information today, right?"

She nodded and handed over her phone. "While we were at dinner." Her mood change began to make sense. I glanced at the text and then hit the highlighted numbers. "I'm sorry my mood messed up our night." She had no idea how wrong she was. Being near her, whether she was in a bad or good mood, would always be a great night for me.

"Don't apologize for things that don't need an apology." I let my finger hover over the call button while we talked.

"But we were having an amazing time, and then I got inside of my head and..."

"I appreciate you thinking of my feelings, Lia," I said, going another route. "But I'm also thinking of yours. You're taking a big step in your life, and it's normal to go through different stages when it comes to your feelings on the matter. You can do that freely with me." She nodded and gave me a small smile. I could see that my words had given her a sense of comfort, and that pleased me. I tapped call and placed the phone on speaker.

"I don't think—"

It began to ring, and she clamped her mouth shut, leaving her unfinished statement hanging in the air.

"*You can do it,*" I mouthed. There was no way I would be giving her any chances to back out of this. She took the phone but kept her wary eyes on mine. The phone continued to ring, and when I thought that it was about to go to voicemail, a female voice picked up.

"Hello?" Magnolia jumped and gave me a frantic look. "Hello?" I waved my hand for her to speak, and she finally found her voice.

"Um... H-hi," she croaked. After clearing her throat, she continued, "I was looking for Gerald."

"Oh," the girl replied. Her voice was soft but inviting. She also sounded...confused and maybe a little intrigued. "May I ask who's calling?"

"I'm... My name is Magnolia and Gerald is my—"

"*Our* father," she finished for Magnolia. "I know who you are."

Magnolia's widened eyes moved from the phone's screen to me. I nodded for her to go on, even though I was a little taken aback that she apparently had another sister. One that she obviously had no idea about.

"You know who I am, but I'm afraid that I don't know you." There was a little more confidence in her voice as she spoke that time. I softly rubbed her neck with one hand while tracing the fingers on her free hand with the other.

"I'm Lily."

"Lily," she whispered. "Another flower."

"Yes," Lily reconfirmed, laughing. "I... I know you didn't call for me, but can we meet? I've always wanted to and I didn't think... Well—"

"I would love to," Magnolia blurted. I could see her visibly releasing a breath. Her shoulders dropped, and she began to worry her bottom lip. "Can you do tomorrow?"

"In the morning, if that's okay."

"That works... Um... is this number the one I can reach you at?"

"It's my personal number," she answered. I furrowed my brows at her admission. Her *personal* number? "I have to go, but you can text me the details, and I'll be there."

"I think my aunt set me up," Magnolia said the second the call ended. We were on the same page with that thought. "She had to have known that it was Lily's number."

"It may be time for another conversation with her. It seems she may know more than she's let on."

"If she knew that we had another sister, why wouldn't she tell us?" Her question wasn't meant for me to answer, so I let her ramble on without interrupting. "What if Lily isn't the only one? And how the hell am I supposed to tell my sisters that there's more to this than we expected? Should I wait, or should I tell them now?" She cursed and shook her head. Magnolia had gone from nervous to shocked to frustrated in such a short time period, and I wanted to do everything I could to ease some of those feelings.

"Do you want my advice?"

"Please."

"You need to tell them before you meet up with her." I was aware that three of the sisters wanted a chance to meet with their father to hash out some things, but the youngest wasn't feeling it at all. She could change her mind once she got this news. "Being honest and upfront is the best policy."

"You're right," she mused. "I don't even know why I'm stressing myself out about it."

"Because you're the oldest and they're your babies," I offered, grabbing her chin. "You want to protect them, and that's honorable, but you can do that while also keeping them in the loop."

"Do you always have to make things sound so easy?" she whispered, leaning over the center console. "Kiss me, please."

I did as she asked, leaving her question unanswered.

"WOW," Magnolia whispered in awe as she walked around my apartment. The open floor plan gave me the pleasure of watching her every move from my spot on the sofa. She moved with purpose, her eyes slowly scanning every piece of art, family picture, and book she could find. Her hands touched it all. She was leaving her mark all over my place, and I was feeling that more than anything. She turned to look at me with a gold-rimmed picture frame clutched in her hands.

"Is this your mom?" She flipped it around for me to see, but I knew from the frame alone that it was indeed my mother.

I nodded.

Magnolia ran her fingers lightly over the glass it was encased in and smiled.

"She's beautiful."

The compliment washed over me, and my heart began to beat against my chest as if it were meant for me. She looked at that picture of my mother with so much understanding dancing in her gaze.

"You guys look alike," she said, glancing up at me. She then turned to place the frame back in its rightful place.

"I took after her, while Nard took after our pops."

"I see that." She moved along the wall to where my DVD collection sat. It was mostly old and new anime series that I enjoyed enough to buy. As she bent over, I tilted my head like it would give me a better view of her ass. The light-colored jeans she wore already looked to be painted on, yet they moved fluidly to accommodate the spreading of her hips.

"You have the good stuff here," she chimed. "*InuYasha* and all the seasons of *Dragon Ball Z*." She wasn't facing me, but I knew she was smiling.

"I take it you're a fan." Her nod was subtle, but I caught it.

"You have *Sailor Moon*!" she screeched, spinning to face me. "All five seasons!"

"It was a gift from Leonard." The kid I knew to be buried deep inside of her was shining through right now. I'd gotten a glimpse of her at Hersheypark. That part of Magnolia was more open to allowing people inside of her world. I wanted to bring that side of her out more often.

"Juniper is going to lose her mind when I tell her you have

this. When we were kids, we would wake up early enough to catch it before school and race home afterward so that we wouldn't miss *Dragon Ball Z*."

Her smile was bright as she placed the set back on the shelf and then sauntered over to me. As she tried to sit, I grabbed her by the waist and pulled her body into my lap.

"Lennox," she breathed, cutting an eye at me. "You can't—"

"What?" I asked, cutting in. "Feel on you? Have you close?"

"I was going to say you can't pull me into your lap and not feel on me." She adjusted her body so that she was straddling me and then wrapped her arms around my neck. "The two go hand in hand, don't they?"

"Something like that." I leaned in and grazed her lips with mine. "You're beautiful."

"I really love hearing you say that."

"Yeah?"

"Mmhm, say it again."

"You're beautiful," I repeated, gripping her ass tightly. "Sexy, fine as fuck, taste like heaven, and this..." I kissed her neck and then ran my tongue along her shoulder blade. "Your skin."

"What about...what about it?" she whispered, kissing my nose.

"Dark like coffee, smooth like butter... It's everything that's beautiful about a Black woman."

"What else is beautiful about Black women?"

"Your strength is the catalyst of who you guys are. Everything about you resorts back to that."

"Sometimes we don't want to be strong."

"And with me, you can take a break whenever you need it." Her eyes danced slowly across my face, and I followed their movement with my own. "If you let me."

"How can you be so open to love after everything you've been through with your ex-wife?"

"My past doesn't define what my future will be like, I do."

"You make it sound so easy." She sighed and looked away from me. I didn't let that last for too long.

I turned her head to face me again and said, "It wasn't easy at all, but I worked on it and myself. I came to terms with what happened, and I moved on."

"And then you met me."

"And then I met you, and I see in you everything I want for myself."

"But I'm—"

"You aren't damaged, Lia."

"Then why do I feel like I am?"

"Because you haven't given me the chance to show you that I'm worthy of all of you. That no matter what you feel about yourself, I don't see that part of you."

"I'm giving you a chance now," she murmured, grinding her hips into my growing erection. "Don't fuck it up."

"I can't promise perfection." I held onto her hips to steady her movements. We had time for that. I wasn't letting her leave without taking every inch of her.

"What can you promise me?"

"Honesty," I started. "Loyalty, my whole heart, and some bomb ass sex." Her head flew back, and she gave me the most melodic laugh I'd ever heard from her.

"Bomb ass sex, huh?" I nodded and smacked her ass. "C-can you give me a taste of what's to come?"

I smiled and lifted us from the couch.

"I can give you that and then some." I pushed us into my bedroom, and her gasp was precisely what I had expected.

ELEVEN

MAGNOLIA

"Oh my God," I muttered after Lennox set me on my feet. I turned in a slow circle, taking in the panoramic view of the city. The light from the night's sky gave his bedroom an almost futuristic glow. I was in awe. "This is..." I paused and moved toward the far left side of his bedroom. Pressing my face to the glass, I looked down at the city below.

"It's what?" he asked, pressing his chest into my back. He looped his arms around me, and I settled into them.

"Serene."

I couldn't stop the feelings that were bubbling up inside of me. Lennox had always made me feel comfortable, but lately, that comfort was becoming more. I wanted to be near him all the time. I craved his conversation and now his touch. This had been happening for months. These feelings had roots to them. The foundation had been built whether I wanted it to be or not. And it was becoming clear that my feelings of him being too good to be true had no validity to them. Lennox was exactly who he presented himself to be. Was this what I had been missing out on all of this time? Was this what falling for someone felt like?

Shit.

Am I falling for Lennox?

"Hey, Lennox?" I turned to face him. His gaze met mine, and my heart began to race.

"Wassup, beautiful?"

"What does, um... What does falling in love feel like?"

Asking him that felt surreal. I'd never been in love, but I wanted to be.

"You've never..." He shook his head and led me to the bed. With a gentle push, I was flat on my back. Seconds later, Lennox was positioned between my thighs and hovering over me. "You've really never been in love?"

"Well...no, not really."

"Have you ever had a serious relationship?" I shrugged.

"I've been in relationships."

"But they were never serious because you run," he theorized. He wasn't necessarily speaking to me anymore. He was analyzing me and letting his inner thoughts spill. "I thought I had you figured out, Lia, but every time I learn something new, it's clear that I don't know anything at all."

"What is it that you think you know about me?" I asked, lifting my body slightly and balancing myself on my elbows. Lennox observed me, his eyes moving across my face to take me in completely. He licked his lips and then hooked his fingers into the hem of my shirt.

"Can I take this off?" he asked with his eyes still penetrating me. I had no idea where he was going with this, but I didn't deny his request. Instead, I lifted my arms and let him remove my shirt. He then took off his own shirt and stood from the bed, taking me with him.

"W-what are you doing?"

"I want you to see something." With my hand in his, we moved toward the right side of his room. "When I moved into this apartment, I picked it because of the view in this room. Nothing else mattered but this. I'm my most creative when I'm in here, sitting in the dark with nothing but moonlight shining through." He pressed his finger to the glass, and my eyes darted to where he was pointing.

"Full moon," I whispered. He nodded and placed my body in front of his. He wrapped his arms around me and held me close. Once again, I settled into the embrace, melting on contact. No man...and I mean *no* man had ever made me feel safe enough to melt in their arms.

"When you think of a full moon, what comes to mind?"

"The end of something," I said. Lennox's hands began to caress me as he spoke.

"I agree to an extent, but I also believe that a full moon is the beginning of something you've been seeking. It means it's done. Signed off on and on its way to you. What do you desire, Lia?"

Now he was unhooking my bra and tossing it aside. His fingers grazed my nipples, but he didn't fully pursue that part of me. He cupped what he could into his palms and moved us closer to the window. I was at a loss for words, but I tried my best to answer him without stammering.

"I desire...happiness."

"And what do you think will make you happy?" His lips were on my neck. He lightly pecked my skin, giving me goosebumps.

"Understanding," I whispered, biting down on my lip.

"Of what?"

"Of who I am and where I come from."

"So meeting your father isn't just about confronting him," he assessed. "It's about figuring out what part of Magnolia Baker came from him."

"I..." I couldn't finish my statement. I kept my gaze locked on the full moon. Was Lennox right? Was that what I was seeking underneath all my anger?

"You don't have to speak, baby, because I understand now." I didn't even think *I* understood. How could he? "Everything you've manifested is yours, Lia."

"What if I don't know what I manifested?"

"You know," he said, kissing my cheek and then spinning me around. "You want understanding. You want happiness." He smiled at me, and I felt weak from the simple gesture. "I think you want love too." Lennox began to work on removing my jeans, and I allowed him while I thought over his assumption. Was it considered an assumption if he was right?

"What makes you think that?"

"It's not something I think, beautiful," he said, rolling my jeans down my thighs until they were at my ankles. I kicked them off and then wrapped my arms around his neck. "I know it's what you want."

"I don't know what love feels like, remember? How can I want something I've never had?"

"How do people want dream jobs they've never worked?" he quipped, leaning in to gently kiss my lips. "We desire things all the time that we've never had. Love falls into that category."

"What does...what does it feel like?" I asked for the second time tonight. He responded by lifting me into his arms and pressing my back against the cold glass. I wrapped my legs around his waist, and he held me in place by gripping my ass.

"It feels like the world is spinning," he started, staring me directly in my eyes. "Like you can't breathe, but in reality, your lungs are clear, and every time you take in a breath, there's one scent that's always there. Your heartbeats quicken every time the person is near. You crave their attention. You want to hear their voice when your day isn't going as planned, and they're the first person you want to speak to when everything is falling into place. When you part from them, you feel this tug in your chest that's begging you to go after them." He paused, his eyes dancing in front of me. Lennox was expressing everything I had been feeling for him. Everything I had once been confused about became clear.

I was falling in love.

I was falling in love with Lennox, and I didn't want to run away from it.

I wanted to run toward it.

I wanted to run toward *him*.

"Do you feel any of that when you're with me, Lia?"

"Yes," I answered truthfully. "I-I feel all of it."

"And how does that make you feel right now?" he asked.

"I fear it, but I want it." He chuckled and smirked.

"See," he said. "Manifesting." And that was the end of that conversation. My body was humming with need, and Lennox could feel it. I could see his own need for me deep in his gaze. He'd managed to get rid of his jeans and boxers with me still perfectly balanced against the glass. "Place your hand over my heart."

I did as he asked and was shocked to find his heart beating out of control.

"That happens when you're near me."

Was he saying...

"I'm falling in love with you too," he said, confirming my thoughts. "And I want to be. I want you, Lia. I want there to be an *us*. I crave that shit."

I couldn't find the words, but that didn't matter. Lennox had other plans for us. He ripped my lace thong from my body and tossed it. Before I could open my mouth to complain, his lips were on mine. This time around, there was nothing gentle about it. He attacked my mouth with all the passion he had obviously been holding back, and I returned the sentiment.

This...

This was everything.

"Please," I begged, grinding my pussy into his erection. My slick lips moved with ease up his length. I wanted him so bad. "Lennox— Oh, shit."

"Fuck," he muttered, biting into the fleshy part of my shoulder. Lennox pushed his way inside of me. And when he was in completely, my body adjusted to his size without complication. Lennox wasted no time, pulling out of me and then dipping back inside with a powerful stroke. I let out a strangled gasp and then arched my body into his.

I was damn near sobbing with desperation.

I needed more, and I wasn't against begging.

"Again, please," I groaned, pushing myself into him. He gave me exactly what I wanted right against the glass. Our bodies moved in sync as he fucked me with no remorse. The sweet-talking professor was gone, leaving me with an animal on a mission. My body knocked against the glass with each stroke.

"You feel so damn good," he groaned in my ear. His words only ignited more fire inside of me.

"Harder," I begged. He took a step back, lifting my body to the tip of his dick. "Yes!" I screamed as he connected us again. *God, yes.* Lennox repeated the soul-snatching move over and over while repeating how wet my pussy was. How I was sucking him in better than anything he'd felt before. The more he spoke, the wetter and louder I became. He was catering to my every need, giving me the deepest strokes while speaking life into me.

"I need that from you," he commanded in a raspy voice. "Give me that orgasm. I feel it."

"Shit." I was outdone. My body reacted to his order, and I couldn't stop it. Before I knew it, my pussy muscles were tightening. My stomach clenched, and I was screaming for God to have mercy on me. "Oh, my God."

"That's right, baby," he coached. "Let it go."

My body went limp, and Lennox's strokes became jerky.

My head popped up, and I blurted, "Cum in my mouth."

That wasn't what you were going to say.

But I didn't back out when Lennox placed me on my feet. I dropped to my knees and wrapped my lips around his dick. All it took were a couple of pulls, and he was releasing his semen down my throat.

"Fuuuck," he groaned, holding onto my head. I stayed in place, knowing he was on the verge of falling over. After a few seconds, he let go and pulled me to my feet. He stared down at me through a hooded gaze. "You are everything I imagined and then some."

Why'd he have to say that?

My heart smiled. How was him talking about my pussy being good making me smile?

Because you're a nasty bitch.

I smirked at the thought as he gathered me into his arms and whispered, "You're mine."

"A SISTER," Daisy repeated.

"Named after a flower," Juniper added, frowning.

"What are the fucking odds of that?" Lilac seethed. She was more upset than anything, and it had everything to do with missing out on knowing our other sister.

"I don't understand," Blossom said. She hadn't said much since I broke the news. I was meeting with Lily in two hours, but I wanted to let them know first, so I'd settled for a group FaceTime call. "Dad had other kids? Is she younger than me?"

"That's a good question," I said. I wouldn't put it past Gerald having outside kids when he was with my mother. "I'll find out when I meet with her."

"I really wish I could meet up with you guys," Daisy said, sighing. "This is too much for us not to be doing it together."

"I think it's best this way. Let me feel her out, and then we'll know if it's a situation worth pursuing."

"Do you think Lori knew about her?"

"I'm almost positive that she did," I replied. "She gave me her number, Juni. Why would she do that without giving me a heads-up?"

We were all silent after the question left my lips. I had a feeling we were all thinking the same thing. Lori didn't want us overthinking this situation, and we would have had we known about Lily beforehand.

"Mags," Juniper called out, tilting her head sideways. "Did you spend the night with Lennox?"

I looked around his bedroom and then down at him. He was still asleep. "What makes you ask that?"

All of my sisters were now sitting up straight and eyeing me curiously.

"Oh my God!" Daisy screeched. "You're still there." I lowered my head to hide my smile only to find Lennox watching me.

"You had sex!" Blossom yelled. "He finally knocked those cobwebs—"

Lennox's deep laughter filled the room, and Blossom clamped her mouth shut.

"He's right there!" they yelled in unison.

"You guys," I groaned. "I'm hanging up now."

"Don't you dare han—"

I ended the call and tossed my phone.

"Please, don't judge them based on the things they say."

"You haven't heard Nard in rare form yet," he said, speaking about his older brother. Lennox wrapped his arms around me and pulled me on top of him. "Good morning, beautiful."

"Good morning," I murmured in reply. I grazed his lips with mine and then planted a big one on them. "I have to head home."

"I know."

He'd acknowledged it, but instead of letting me go, he tightened his grip on me.

"Lennox—"

"You can spare me ten minutes."

"What's happening in those ten minutes?" I asked, burying my face into his neck. The faint scent of his signature cologne was there. I took another whiff and groaned.

"Nothing," he said. "I want to hold you."

I didn't have the energy to fight him on it, and even if I did, I wouldn't have. Being in his arms was the best feeling. I never wanted to be without them around me.

"This is nice."

"Nice enough for you to come back later tonight?"

My answer came without any hesitation. "Definitely." I was working the store for Juniper today, so my night would be a little longer than usual, but that didn't matter to me. Seeing Lennox again...being close to him...getting to know him more. That was important to me.

"Are you nervous about your meeting with Lily?"

I sighed and snuggled closer. "A little, but it has to be done, right?"

"It does," he replied, kissing my cheek. "I could come with you."

"But...don't you have class?"

"Not on Tuesdays."

"I totally forgot." I lifted my head so I could see his eyes. "As much as I appreciate you offering, I have to do this alone."

He gripped my chin with his right hand and pulled me close. "If you need me..."

He let his voice trail off and kissed me. I knew he was going for simple, but I wanted more. I deepened the kiss, slipping my tongue into his mouth. We lay in each other's arms for what felt like hours, kissing like two teenagers. Eventually, Lennox broke the contact and said, "You better go."

"I better," I agreed, nodding. I still needed to go home, shower, and change. I reluctantly climbed out of bed and began to gather my clothes. After slipping into my fit from the night before, I leaned into the mattress and kissed Lennox one last time.

As I neared the bedroom door, he called out to me. I glanced over my shoulder just as he was saying, "If you need me..."

Smiling, I gave him a nod and then made my exit.

About an hour and a half later, I was whipping my car into a spot outside of Abner's Cheesesteaks. I took a few deep breaths and then opened the door. It was a chilly morning but still no snow. The temperature had dropped drastically, so I made sure to bundle up more than I had been. With my phone and wallet clutched in my hand, I stepped into the nearly empty restaurant. A couple was sitting near the door, and then sitting at a table near the back was a girl with long straight hair and dark skin just like mine. I slowly made my way to her.

As I neared the table, she looked up, and I stopped dead in my tracks. Her and Blossom looked like twins, and I hadn't been expecting that at all.

"Hi," she spoke, standing. I snapped out of my trance and took her hand.

"Sorry," I said. "You just look a lot like my baby sister." She gave me a half-smile, and we took our seats. "You haven't been here long, have you?"

"No, I was running a little late." I nodded and picked up the menu. It was a way for me to get my thoughts together. I knew this menu like the back of my hand already, and I always ordered the same steak when I allowed myself to indulge. That wouldn't be changing today.

"I'm really nervous," she whispered. I glanced up at her and felt my heart tugging. That instinct I got with my sisters had just hit me. I wanted her to be as comfortable as possible, so I set my menu down and smiled at her.

"It's cool," I said, waving my hand. "I was a little nervous too." She nodded and gave me a smile back. I could see her shoulders relaxing, and that made me happy.

"I figured... I guess I thought you guys wouldn't want anything to do with me."

"How long have you known we existed?"

"A couple of years," she replied, lowering her head. "I, um... My aunt... Your aunt—"

"Our aunt," I corrected. "Lori, right?" She nodded. I guess I had my answer on if she knew about Lily this entire time.

"She told me about you guys when I reached out to her a few years ago."

"So you hadn't known about her until then?"

"Y-yes. I... My mom told me about her, and I wanted to know her, so I begged for her number. She didn't want to give it to me at first, but eventually, she did." She gave me a bright smile and then said, "I can be pretty convincing when I want to be."

Laughing, I said, "That sounds like a Fredericks trait."

"You guys don't have his last name." It wasn't a question.

"Lori helped us change them to our mother's maiden name when we moved in with her." After Gerald had signed away his rights, I felt like carrying his last name would be pointless. When I asked Lori about helping me change it, my sisters revealed that they wanted the same as well. To us, a last name was about carrying on the legacy of your father, and by law, he wasn't even that anymore.

"I see." That was where the conversation went dark. She was closing herself off from me, and I could visibly see it happening. I understood how that came across since she donned his last name, but we wanted to know her. The man that connected us wouldn't stop that.

"That doesn't make us any less sisters," I said. "We obviously share the same DNA. It's just... Gerald was never there for us. He was already out of the house before my mother passed. He then signed over his parental rights after she was already gone. That's how we ended up with Lori."

Her eyes widened, and a tiny gasp left her lips.

"I—I'm sorry. Lori didn't explain the history with you guys to me. I thought..." She paused and pushed her glasses up on her face. "I thought maybe your mom... Never mind."

"She didn't keep us from him. He chose to leave us."

"I guess I don't understand because I don't know the same man that you do." I nodded. I understood, alright. "He was...he was there for me."

There was something about her using his name in the past tense that unnerved me.

"Was?"

"He, um... He's not dead," she rushed out. "Just...on life support."

"Excuse me?"

Her eyes were clouded with tears, but I didn't have it in me to cry.

Life support?

That was how this would end?

It was disheartening. I had so much to say to him. The awake and comprehensive version of him.

"Life support," she repeated, wiping her eyes. "He had a seizure at work, and no one was around. He lay there for an hour without any help. By the time the paramedics got to him, he—"

"Please don't finish that," I said, cutting her off. "I'm sorry about your father."

"He's *our* father." I furrowed my brows and squinted my eyes at her. Was she serious? I may have called Gerald *my* father when I talked about him to my sisters, but to the rest of the world, he was Gerald to me, and that's how it would stay. "Look, I know that he wasn't there for you or the others, but he's dying. He's basically already dead, and his fiancée is taking him off life support soon. I was going to reach out to you, but you got to me first. I think that...maybe it's time to make amends."

I stared at her like she'd grown two heads.

Make *amends*.

That wasn't on my agenda at all, but instead of voicing that, I changed the subject. While I didn't care for her trying to push this on me, I still wanted to know more about her.

"How old are you?" I asked. Lily gave me a curious look before sighing.

"Twenty-one." Definitely younger than Blossom.

"Are you in school?" She nodded and smiled.

"It's my senior year at Penn." That made me smile. I loved an educated young Black woman. "Where did you go to school?"

"NYU."

"I tried getting that out of Lori, but she only told me your guys' names and ages." I laughed.

"Lori set us up."

"She did, but I'm glad she went about it that way," she whispered. "I want to know my sisters. That's the one thing I hate about our...my father." I appreciated her switching that up for me. "He took away my right to know you guys and Lori."

"Do you know why he didn't tell you about Lori?"

"Something about a fight." She shrugged. "I didn't ask details." I tapped the menu in front of me and then glanced at the area where we would place an order.

"How about we go order and then finish this conversation while we eat?" She nodded, and we walked to the front of the restaurant. After placing our orders and watching them make the cheesesteaks in front of us, we paid and retreated to our table. I bit into my chicken cheesesteak and groaned. That first bite was always the best.

"I would really love to meet the other girls," Lily spoke after taking a sip of her soda. "I know I probably came off really strong when it came to making amends, but I've learned the hard way that life is too short to be angry."

"That's easier said than done."

"I know, and I can't imagine what it must have felt like to be denied the love of a father, but..." She paused and shook her head. "You know what... I'm not being completely honest."

Her partial confession stilled me. I set my steak down and leaned back in my chair.

"How so?"

"Gerald... He wasn't really a part of my life until a year before I got in contact with Lori. I hadn't known him growing up at all. My mother only told me who he was after I started asking more questions than usual. She gave me a name and number, and I reached out to him."

"So..." I took a deep breath. Lily was trying every bit of my patience. I was trying to be understanding, but she was making it hard. "Why lie?"

"I wanted... I don't know what I wanted."

"Everyone knows what they want, Lily," I pushed out. "Whether it's consciously or subconsciously."

"I wanted to know my sisters, but I didn't want us to bond over *him* not playing a role in any of our lives."

"You could've done that by being honest from the very beginning."

"Did I mess up?" she asked, tucking a piece of her hair behind her head.

"Not enough that I want to get up and walk away," I said. I slightly understood her fear. I also had that fierce instinct to protect her. It was the same I had with my sisters. She was lucky it was me here and not Juniper or Blossom. They would have left her sitting there and never looked back. "But let's be clear, I don't like being lied to. I don't like being played, and I won't tolerate it from anyone who will be in my life. This is the only chance you will get, so please don't mess it up. Just be yourself."

She threw her hands up and said, "I promise that won't ever happen again."

I eyed her for a minute and saw nothing but sincerity in her gaze.

"Alright, now tell me the truth."

TWELVE

LENNOX

"Oh, shit!" Devin shouted, covering his mouth with his fist. "If it isn't Professor Ivy League."

"Come on, man, what I tell you about calling me that?"

I stepped further into the bar he owned, and he met me halfway. Devin Booker was one of my good friends from my undergrad days at Villanova. We were dorm mates for the first two years and then had an off-campus apartment together the last two. I was a bit of a recluse in school. I preferred having my face buried in a book most of the time, but Devin made sure I had fun too.

Any trouble that I got into was because of him. He was also the reason why I met Nina when I did.

"I like the nickname," he said, laughing. "What brings you to my place of business? We usually meet up on card nights, so if you're here outside of that, then I know something's up."

He tossed his head in the direction of his office, and I followed him. Booker's Bar & Grill was a hot spot on South Street. When Devin came to me about opening it, I supported his business venture. He didn't ask for money, just for a friend to pitch in on opening night. Devin was real business-savvy and good with numbers. I knew that anything he put his mind to would become a gem, and that's exactly what happened.

"I was wondering if I could borrow the bar for two Sundays from now." We entered his office, and I took a seat on the black leather couch he had stationed on the left side of the room. Devin sat behind his desk and threw me a thoughtful look.

"You're always asking the weirdest shit without giving the full details first." I couldn't do anything but laugh because he was right. "Give me the rundown of what you have in mind, and we'll work it out."

And that right there was the reason me and Devin would always be solid. I never needed to explain further. He'd always look out, just as I would if he needed it. I explained what I had in mind, and as I talked, his smile grew wider and wider.

"You met someone?"

"I told you about her," I reminded him. I didn't see Devin often, but we spoke on the regular. It didn't matter if it was through a phone call or text, we always checked up on each other. "Magnolia."

"Oh, shit," he cursed. "The flower. I didn't think..."

"Yeah, me either, but shit is moving in that direction. It was as if one minute she wasn't ready, and the next she was." I wasn't complaining, though.

"And you're ready for that?" Now he was going into therapist mode. I sliced a hand through the air, and he chuckled.

"Don't go all 'I'm a licensed therapist' on me, man." Along with owning a bar, Devin was a therapist. He didn't necessarily use his degree, but to appease his family, he took clients once a week at his father's practice.

"It's in me, but seriously. Is that—"

"Yes. I'm more than sure," I said, leaning my head back and shutting my eyes. "I'm falling for her. Hard."

"Alright, well, the place is yours on Sunday."

"Nina is pregnant," I blurted. The words felt like fire on my tongue, but getting it out was needed. When Devin didn't respond, I lifted my head to find him staring at me with his mouth slightly ajar. "And getting married."

"Nox, I thought you were saying she's pregnant by you."

"Is that why you were looking like you saw a ghost?"

"I was trying to figure out when you became a fuck boy," he quipped, laughing. "Had me worried for a minute."

"You know me better than that. I don't double back." Devin nodded, but the expression on his face told me he had questions. "Is it weird that I don't feel anything about it?"

"Are you sure that you don't?"

"I mean..." I paused to think over my answer. "It feels weird saying it, but other than that, no. I don't have any bad feelings."

"Then it's not weird," he said, shrugging. "It just proves that you've moved on."

I wasn't sure if Devin was right, but his assumption sounded good enough for me at this moment. And when I thought of Magnolia and the look on her face when she realized that she was falling for me... There was shock in her beautiful gaze, but relief followed. She was relieved to be falling for me. In that instance, our feelings were the same.

"Let's go over what I'll need for Sunday." Devin nodded and pulled out a notebook.

An hour later, I was leaving Devin's bar and heading to the grocery store. I wanted to make dinner for Magnolia, but I had no idea what to make. After tapping the steering wheel a few times, an idea sparked.

"Call Samir," I spoke to my car. The automated voice spoke back, confirming what I said, and then it began to ring.

"Wassup, Lenny?" I grimaced but didn't correct him.

"I need to talk to your wife."

"Nigga...you can't speak first?" His tone held a hint of amusement in it, and I chuckled. I was tripping.

"My bad," I said. "I got a lot on my mind. I'm trying to figure out what to make Lia for dinner."

"Y'all situation changed, or is this a friendly dinner?"

"Our situation changed."

"Mmmm," he hummed. A few seconds later, he was talking in a low whisper to someone, and then Brynlee's soft voice filled my car.

"Hey, Lennox," she greeted. Brynlee had this warm air about her. Her spirit was pure and comforting. When I first met her, I was drawn to how down to earth she was. It made perfect sense that she and Samir fell for each other the way they did. "Samir says you want to know what to make Mags for dinner."

"Yeah, I realized that I don't know what her favorite meal is."

"To be honest... Actually, hold please." The line filled with silence, and then a few seconds later, two female voices were speaking at once.

"Nova, you there?"

"I'm here," Nova chimed in. She sounded as if she were eating, and I couldn't help but laugh. "Whoa, whose deep laughter is that cause it ain't Samir, and Elijah is sitting next to me."

"Lennox," I revealed, laughing. Nova was the complete contrast of Brynlee. Her aura was more lively. It was as if she were having a party in her mind at all times. She was also very spiritual. I never needed to hear her speak to know that about her. She moved in a way that spoke to who she was.

"Ah... Lennox, the wordsmith."

"Is that what y'all call me?" Brynlee's giggles were my answer. "I only speak from my heart, and I don't say anything special."

"It doesn't seem special because you're speaking how you feel in the most honest way possible, but to Mags, your words mean everything."

"Every time you tell her she's beautiful, she falls a little more," Brynlee added.

"She is beautiful," I said. "I'm only telling her—"

"The truth," they said simultaneously. "We know."

"What can I do for you, Lennox?" Nova asked.

"What's Magnolia's favorite food?"

"She loves sweet and savory things. Lilac makes these honey garlic wings that she loves, but she has a specific recipe for them that I don't have."

What was it with these women and chicken?

"But you can get it," I said. I whipped my car into a spot outside of Fresh Grocer and leaned back in my seat.

"You want us to finesse Lilac's recipe from her so you can make it for her sister." I could hear Elijah laughing in the background.

"You have no idea how serious Lilac is about her food," Brynlee murmured. "But we can always add her to the call."

"I—"

"Oh, great idea," Nova chirped. "One second." I had no way of knowing what I'd just gotten myself into, but there was no getting out of it at this point.

"The precious Lilac Baker has entered the chat," Lilac announced. "What can I do for you beauties today?"

"It's more so about what you can do for me," I responded, getting straight to it. What I'd learned from Magnolia was that Lilac was a straight shooter. She was a 'say what you mean and mean what you say' type of chick. There was no need for me to skate around what I wanted.

"With a voice like that—"

"Lilac, that voice belongs to your sister's man," Brynlee cut in.

"Oh, damn," she cursed. "My bad... What can I do for you that has me summoned to a group call?"

"I heard you make Magnolia's favorite dish."

"Honey garlic wings," she said. "She loves it. Do you need me to make them for her?"

"I was hoping you'd be kind enough to let me have the recipe so that I can make them for her myself."

Silence.

That was what I received, and for a minute, I thought I had my answer, but then she spoke.

"Here's the thing," she started. "If I give it to you, then I need something in return."

"And what might that be?"

"I need to know that my big sister is safe with you. That she'll never have to worry about being hurt like…" Her voice trailed off, but I knew where she was going with her statement.

"I would never abandon her."

"Typically, I would ask for more reassurance, but I believe you, so I will send you the recipe. After you make it, I need pictures so I can upload them to my blog."

"I can do that for you," I said, smiling. I would do anything to get that damn recipe. I probably could've googled one, but she would know the difference. Magnolia was the type that paid attention to detail, and I didn't want to fuck this up. Not her favorite meal.

"Well, I have to go. I have an event I'm cooking for tomorrow, and I need to prepare. I'll send that to you, Lennox." The girls said their goodbyes, and then Lilac was gone.

"Well, that was easier than I thought it would be," Nova said, sounding like her mouth was full of food again. "And since we got that out of the way, Lennox, take care of my friend. She deserves the world. And with that, I'm gone."

"Lennox, you be good to her," Brynlee murmured before ending the call. I never planned on being anything but good to her, I thought. Before exiting my truck, I sent Magnolia a text.

> I can't stop thinking about your beautiful ass face.

FOR THE LAST HOUR, I've been prepping the meal for Magnolia and me. After cleaning and seasoning the chicken, I spread the wings onto a pan covered in parchment paper. I placed the pan into the preheated oven, washed my hands, and then grabbed my phone to go over the sauce recipe that Lilac texted me one more time. I realized after receiving the message from an unknown number that I hadn't given her mine. She must have gotten it from Brynlee. I read the message attached to the recipe and laughed. I was more certain now than I was before that Lilac was the firecracker between the five of them.

> If you fuck this up, don't tell my sister you used my shit. It's bad for business, so make me proud.
>
> 1/4 cup water
>
> 1 tbsp molasses
>
> 3 tbsp honey
>
> 6 cloves garlic finely minced
>
> 1 tsp onion powder
>
> 1 tbsp brown sugar packed

I glanced at the ingredients I had set out on the counter and checked each off the list for the fifth time. After confirming I had everything I needed, I read the rest of her text.

> Mix the ingredients together in a bowl. Pour the mixture in a small saucepan and over medium heat, bring the sauce to a boil, then reduce heat and simmer until mixture reduces and thickens about 5 minutes; it should reduce to about half. After this, you should be ready to pour over your wings. I prefer to put them back in the oven to let them bake into the skin. Save a little of the sauce so that she can dip the wings. That's her favorite part. Good luck!

I had pretty much memorized what to do next, but I wanted to be sure I had it down. Like she'd stated, I couldn't fuck this up. I was a good cook, but damn, was I nervous. I had about thirty minutes before the wings would be done baking, so I preoccupied myself by calling my father.

"Son," he answered just as he always does.

"Hey, pop." I plopped down on the couch and picked up the remote. "How are you?"

"Old and cranky on most days." The gruffness in his voice put me at ease.

"I agree with the cranky part, but I think you may be getting younger." He laughed, and I swear I could see his mustache moving in my head.

"Tell that to these knees of mine, and when you're done, get on with why you really called." I forgot how well he was at reading Leonard and me, even when we weren't standing directly in front of him. "Go on."

"About mom," I started. "Have you considered what we talked about?"

"I have, and I think it's time too, but before it happens, she and I need to work out some things." When he stopped talking, I knew that meant he was done with the topic. That also meant that he was taking things into his own hands, and Leonard and I could stand down.

"I understand," I said. "Loud and clear."

He grumbled something under his breath and then said, "Who is Magnolia?"

"Who told you about her?"

"A four-year-old who seems to be obsessed with flowers."

"Ah. Kendall heard us talking about her when I was there," I said. "She's a friend. More than that."

"So, your girlfriend?"

"I'm going to go out on a limb here and say yes."

I would have a definite answer after tonight. I wanted to build with Magnolia, and it was important to me that she understood what that meant.

"You let me know if you still have that limb after you actually ask her."

"Come on, pop," I said, laughing. "Have faith in your dear old boy."

"Oh, I do," he confirmed. "Always have. Hopefully, this one isn't like that ex-wife of yours."

My pop had never been a fan of Nina, and he never had a problem voicing his distaste.

"She's nothing like Nina."

"Then you won't mind me meeting her."

"I wouldn't mind... Her and I just need to work through some things." I was throwing his words back at him, and I was positive he'd catch on and understand. Magnolia could still be a flight risk, and I needed to be sure that she was down for this ride with me. Through thick and thin.

"I understand," he mimicked. "Loud and clear." My line beeped, and I pulled my phone away from my ear to see who was calling.

"Speaking of Magnolia," I muttered. "This is her on my other line. I'll call you tomorrow, pop, I love you."

"I love you too, son."

I quickly clicked over and greeted her. "What's good, pretty lady?"

She laughed and replied with, "Sometimes you speak, and I forget that you teach English."

"I'm educated, but I still grew up in the hood."

"You and Samir didn't live in the same neighborhood?"

"Nah," I replied, flipping through the channels before landing on ESPN. "We went to the same school, but his parents were a little more well off than mine."

"I see," she murmured. "So my man is a little hood. I like that."

Her words hit me, and a smile stretched across my face before I could stop it.

"Oh, shoot. I have to go, Lennox. I'm supposed to be helping the girls on the floor so we can close up early. I just wanted you to know that I'll be headed to you soon, love."

She hung up, and I set my phone down with the same silly smile on my face. Damn, I felt like a kid in a candy store. We still had some things to work through, but I was more confident now about her position in my life then I had been ten minutes ago.

I turned up the television and walked into the kitchen to check my wings.

"Running back Semaj Tanneson seen leaving the Giants facility today. What do we think of this? After the Giants season ended, we heard rumors of him voicing his concerns about how the season went to the front office. What are your thoughts, Yari?" I cut my eyes at the TV to get a look at the sportscaster, Yari Logan. She was the only woman sitting at the round table, and in my opinion, she was the most insightful. I liked hearing her thoughts on all things sports, but especially football.

"I personally think that Semaj has a right to speak his piece," Yari stated. *"He was the reason the Giants went as far as they did, and he may be new to the team, but he isn't a rookie. That's a vet we're speaking on right now. Respect that."*

"Has your husband given his thoughts on it?"

Yari was married to the retired future Hall of Famer Montana Stephens. He was one of my favorite players when he did play, and now his brother was dominating the game.

"Now, you know I don't disclose my husband's thoughts on television. I'm sure he'll speak on this topic when his show airs."

She smiled and winked at the camera.

Laughing, I focused my attention on making the sauce. Magnolia said she'd be here soon, and I wanted everything to be done beforehand. ESPN would have to wait.

Holy shit! Those look amazing.

> Definitely posting these pictures on my blog tonight.

I CHUCKLED at Lilac's text messages and shot her back one that said:

> 'preciate you looking out.

I checked the time and then grabbed the bottle of white wine from the fridge to pour two glasses. I glanced in the oven at the chicken and licked my lips at the smell. My stomach grumbled, and I shut the stove to stop myself from tasting a piece without her. After a few minutes of looking around the kitchen with a million thoughts running through my mind, I walked away. I shook my head. I was tripping. Magnolia told me she was twenty minutes away—I glanced at my Apple Watch—fifteen minutes ago.

My phone rang and thinking it was Magnolia, I picked up.

"Yo."

"L-Lennox."

I frowned.

"Nina?" I questioned, pulling my phone away from my ear. "What number are you calling me from?"

"I, um... It's new."

"Oh, alright." I walked into my bedroom and pulled my shirt off. "Wassup?"

She didn't sound like herself, but I didn't have time to baby Nina right now. It was always something, and I was getting tired of the random calls whenever she felt like she *needed* me. I grabbed a new shirt after tossing the old one into the laundry basket in my closet. I'd already showered, but my other shirt smelled like I'd been slaving over a stove.

"Can you talk, and before you say no, it's not like that... I just need some advice."

"I'm listening."

"James broke things off with me," she started. I almost rolled my eyes, but I caught myself. "I guess I just want to know if I'm really that bad of a person that everyone leaves me?"

Her question put me in an instant bad mood. Why was I being asked this?

"I can't tell you why James left you, Nina," I said calmly. "What I can tell you is that you aren't a bad person. You just make bad decisions that ultimately have severe consequences."

"We could have worked our issues out," she cried. "W-we were in love, and you—"

"You cheated." I stated the obvious as simply as possible. "There was no coming back from that for me. We've discussed this more times than I've wanted to. Why are we having the conversation again?"

"I miss you," she whispered.

"You're also pregnant," I reminded her as I walked toward the door where knocking had just commenced. With my phone still pressed to my ear, I pulled the door open and came face to face with the finest woman I'm sure I'll ever encounter. Magnolia's beauty was unmatched. "On top of that, I'm seeing someone that I plan on marrying one day, so I need this to be the last time you call without a legit reason."

"Lenn—"

I hung up and snatched Magnolia into the apartment. I shut the door and grabbed her bag from her hand.

She eyed me curiously and then asked, "Care to share?"

"Just setting my ex-wife straight before this thing between us becomes more than what it is now." I gripped her now-free hand in mine and pulled her toward my bedroom.

"Oh," she muttered, frowning. "That was her on the phone?"

"It was." I dropped her bag on the floor in my closet and then gathered her into my arms. "Are you jealous?"

Her eyes widened, and then she pushed me. Her goal had been to get me to let her go, but I wasn't going for that.

"Why would I be jealous?" She was trying her hardest to play it off, but what she was feeling was written all over her face.

"You tell me, Lia." I gripped her chin and then planted a kiss on her glossed lips. "This pout on your face, as cute as it is, is telling me otherwise."

"Okay," she said, sighing. "I'm jealous, and I felt the same when you said she visited you at Penn."

"I'm flattered." I kissed her lips again. "But you have no reason to be jealous. What I had with Nina is over, and what I have with you is my top priority. *You* are my top priority."

"Do you promise?"

"With all my heart," I said. "Do you want to shake or kiss on it?" The corners of her mouth lifted and spread out so far I almost lost it. "Why are you so damn beautiful?"

"Which question should I answer first?" She tilted her head at me, and I decided to answer the first question for both of us by going in for my third kiss.

"The second one."

"I'm beautiful because God made me this way," she joked, spinning on her heels and leaving the closet. "I smell food."

I followed behind her with my eyes glued to her ass. She was rocking a pair of grey leggings that had her looking thicker than usual.

"I might have cooked something," I said. We entered the kitchen, and I picked up an oven mitt to grab the pan from the oven. As I set the pan on the stove, I chuckled at the wild curls that were hanging over my shoulder.

"Holy moley," she exclaimed, pressing her head into my neck. "Is that what I think it is?"

Grabbing her by the waist, I pulled her body in front of mine. "What do you think it is?" I asked, reaching around her to grab a wing.

"I know my sister's wings when I see them, but the question is, how did you get the recipe? I've been trying for..." She paused and bit into the piece I placed in front of her lips. "Oh my goodness, Lennox." She took the wing from my hand and finished it off.

"I take it you like them," I guessed, stepping back so that I could lean up against the counter. She turned her body to face me with her eyes squinted.

"How'd you get Lilac to give you her recipe?" She shook her head. "How did you even get in touch with her?" She was talking to me but also reaching for another piece of chicken.

"I called Brynlee to ask what your favorite dish was, she called Nova, and then she called Lilac." I grabbed the bowl of extra sauce and popped the top off it. "Here." Her eyes lit up as she broke the wing apart and dipped one half into the sauce.

"I don't know," she started with a full mouth. "These might taste better than the chef's."

"We won't tell her that." Magnolia's eyes landed on the wine I had poured, and she glanced back at me.

"Is that for me too?" I nodded and handed her a glass. I watched her gulp down half of it and laughed.

"Let's put these in a bowl and head in the living room." She nodded but grabbed my hand to stop me from moving.

"Thank you for this, Lennox," she whispered, closing the space between us. "It really means a lot that you endured a three-way call with my friends and sister to find out my favorite meal."

"I would do it again if I needed to." I wrapped my arm around her and tugged her body closer. "I'm invested in knowing everything about you, Lia. If I have to go through your friends and sisters to figure you out, then I will, but I would like it if I can come straight to the source."

"I want that."

"My girl?"

"Your girl, yeah."

I nodded and let that boulder on my shoulder roll off. She was ready.

THIRTEEN

MAGNOLIA

I couldn't believe Lennox had actually gotten Lilac's honey garlic sauce recipe.

She protected it with her life, so that meant he must have impressed her in some way, shape, or form. I couldn't resist texting what had transpired in the group chat I had with the girls and my sisters. My phone had been lighting up for the last ten minutes with messages. I truly had a hilarious circle.

Juniper: You gave him your recipe???

Nova: But did it turn out good?

Bomb as hell.

Daisy: I'm slightly offended, but also I'm here for it. Conflicted for sure.

Lilac: You guys, please stop whining. I was just trying to help him win our sister's heart, that's all. Please forgive me.

> Blossom: Just make me some, and all will be forgiven.

> Elena: I'm not offended, but I'd still like some.

I giggled at their banter and set my phone down.

"The girls are arguing over Lilac giving you her recipe," I told Lennox. He was standing in the doorway of his office, watching me. We had eaten every wing along with the sweet potato fries that he made with them. He chuckled and then licked his lips. I looked him up and down and then settled my gaze on his very visible dickprint. "I was thinking—"

"What I tell you about that?" The authority in his tone gave me chills. And just that quick, I was turned on and ready to go.

"You need me to know." He moved toward me, and I bit down on my lip. The man had swag and the personality to back it up.

"Tell me what you need," he directed. "Tell me what you know that you need."

"I know that I want you to fuck me." I lifted my hoodie over my head and tossed it. "I know that I need to come." Hooking my fingers into my leggings, I pulled them off. The second the thin fabric was out of my hands, he was on me.

"Tell me about your meeting with your long-lost sister." How did he expect me to speak when he had his lips on my neck and his fingers inside of my thong?

His thumb grazed my clit, and I gasped. "Was she what you thought she would be?"

"I—she was... S-she looks just like Blossom," I managed to get out.

"Mmm," he hummed, licking my neck and then sucking on the spot. He slipped a finger inside of me, and then another.

"Lenn—"

"Finish telling me." Truthfully, I didn't want to talk about my meeting with Lily. She was a sweet girl with a good head on her shoulders, and our conversation after she decided to be honest had been great. I learned that our father and her mom dated for a few months but broke things off early on. Her mother found out she was pregnant with Lily a few months later and reached out to Gerald. He, in return, told her that he didn't want children even though, at that point, he'd already had five. The rest of the story was insignificant to me. The only thing that mattered was that I needed to break the news to my sisters about him being on life support.

"There's nothing to tell," I muttered, lifting my hips to meet the stroke of his fingers. The orgasm I so desperately wanted was bubbling at the surface. I was close. "Except that... Oh, God."

"Go ahead and let it go, baby," he coached in a whisper. The sounds of my pussy juices clashing with his fingers sounded throughout his apartment. "Music to my ears."

I let go.

Hard.

"Fuck. Fuck. Fuck!"

"That was just the appetizer," he said, smiling down at me. "But before we go any further, finish that statement."

"My deadbeat father is dying."

Lennox frowned and leaned back a little. I missed the closeness of his body immediately. "On life, support to be exact."

"That's... You good?" The mischievous glint that was once in his gaze was now replaced with worry. Was he thinking that I wasn't doing well because of a man who was only a part of the first nine years of my life? Did he think I was sad because he was basically already dead? Why should I be? He didn't want me. He signed his rights away quicker than I could yell, "I need you. *We* need you."

"I'm fine," I snapped, pushing him away from me. "Good riddance." I stood from the couch and went for my clothes. As I slipped my shirt over my head, I could see the confusion written all over Lennox's face. I pulled my leggings on and walked toward his bedroom. I had this intense urge to run. To go home and curl up in my bed. But I was fighting it because I wanted to be here too. I wanted Lennox. He pulled something out of me that made me want to face my fears head-on. So I compromised with myself. Instead of leaving the apartment, I simply ran off to his room. I knew he'd follow.

"Let me know where I went wrong?" His voice was soft. Soothing even. I pressed my forehead against the cold glass and stared down at the street. Well...what I could see of it. We were high up, and everything looked so small down below. Like tiny ants.

"Why should I feel something about him dying soon? I shouldn't feel anything, and I haven't all day." I turned to face Lennox, and he was standing on the other side of his massive bedroom with his back pressed against the window. "He doesn't deserve that kind of reaction from me."

"You're right," he agreed, nodding. "He doesn't deserve that."

"Then why would you ask me if I'm okay? Why wouldn't I be?" I knew I sounded crazy, but it was how I was feeling. Why did he have to ask me that? He'd triggered me. I was triggered by the question, and now I didn't know how I felt. Now I wanted to cry because I didn't get to cuss the stupid son of a bitch out for abandoning my sisters and me. For making amends with his youngest daughter but never feeling the need to find the five he had before her. How was any of that fair?

"I asked because deep down, we're all our younger selves." He pushed his body away from the window and slowly walked to me. "It doesn't matter that we're grown, with careers, bills, and real-life problems. None of that shit matters when something takes us back to when we had no care in the world."

"He doesn't deserve me," I whispered, lowering my head.

"And I'm not refuting that, Lia. I agree with you. I agree with the twenty-nine-year-old you completely, but I also feel for that nine- and fifteen-year-old girl who was shot down twice by the man who was supposed to love her first. By the man who, at one point, had shown that love and then snatched it away."

I wrapped my arms around myself and bit down on my lip.

"I didn't deserve that."

"You didn't, baby," he replied, lifting my head. My vision was clouded with tears, but so was his. He was feeling my pain and taking it as his own. "None of you did, but it happened, and now you need to give your younger self what she needs to heal."

"I don't think I can."

"You can do whatever you want, pretty lady." He wiped away the tear that slipped and then kissed the spot. "You're strong. You have the heart of a lion, Magnolia Baker. I knew it the moment we met. Just like I knew you'd be mine after that first conversation. I see you. I feel you. I understand you."

Lennox spoke to a part of me that no man ever had. I heard him. My inner child heard him. As a whole, we understood what needed to be done, and it was because of this man. Because he took his time to penetrate my soul and make me see that I didn't need to hide behind my barriers. That facing my fears didn't mean I was giving in. It just meant that I was doing what was best for me.

"I— I—"

"Shhh, it's alright," he murmured, pulling me close. "Give me the tears, and then we'll figure out the rest later."

Figuring out the rest later sounded good. So, I did what he asked and released the tears that I'd been holding in for so long. They all came spilling out right on Lennox's shoulder, and he held me the entire time, whispering how strong I was in my ear while holding me close to his heart.

"DID YOU KNOW?" I asked my aunt.

Her eyes were darker than usual, and she looked as if she hadn't been sleeping. I was sitting in my living room, waiting for my sisters to arrive. I'd called a group meeting, and I knew the moment they got here, chaos would ensue. They hated being summoned, but more importantly, they hated not knowing why. Before they got here, I needed Lori to answer some questions for me. Talking on the phone wasn't enough, so I FaceTimed her so I could get a clear view of her.

"I knew that you had a sister, yes."

"Auntie, why did you let me call her without telling me what was what?"

"You have more of an open mind when you don't know all the specifics."

"You may be right, but that leaves me to explain what I've learned to the girls." I huffed and laid my head back. "This is already a lot for me, and now I have to take on their feelings too."

"You don't have to take on anything, Magnolia," she fussed. "Your sisters are grown with lives of their own. You don't have to be that motherly figure twenty-four-seven anymore."

I lifted my head and began to say, "I never acted as if—"

"Don't flatter me, niece. I took care of you girls, but you were who they listened to and went to for everything. I only pulled you out of a bad situation."

"No, you raised us to be amazing young women; that's what you did."

"I know what I did, but I'm also acknowledging the role that fifteen-year-old girl took on."

I sighed and looked away from the camera.

"How am I supposed to tell them he's basically dead?"

"You tell them, and you let the chips fall where they may."

"What happened to you and Gerald?"

She chuckled and pulled the hat she was wearing off her head.

"Lily's mother happened," she said. "She was one of my best friends, and we kept in touch when I left Philly. She came to visit me one weekend and told me that she was dating Gerald. I asked if she knew that he had five children he wasn't taking care of, and she hadn't known. Francesca went back home and broke things off with him, but somehow, she hated me for disclosing the information to her. Gerald and I still spoke, but after that, we had a big blowup, and that was it." She rolled her eyes and then laughed again. "I'd already lost most of my family, so it didn't matter that I'd lost him too."

"There's more to that story."

"One that I never plan on telling, so please don't ask again."

"Hello, Mags!" I could hear the rest of my sisters after Blossom yelled out for me.

"It looks like you have some news to break," Lori said. "If you need me, I'm here." I nodded, and we hung up. I wanted to talk a little longer, but there was no point. I didn't think she'd ever reveal what happened to her, and who was I to try and get it out of her?

My sisters came sauntering into the living room one by one, all with curious expressions on their faces. I waved for them to sit down, and they did as I asked.

"Alright," Daisy said in that soft voice of hers. "What is this about because I have this feeling that it isn't good news."

"Same," Juniper co-signed. "I've had this bad feeling in my gut all day." Blossom and Lilac both nodded in agreement, but neither ever opened their mouths. I decided not to waste any time and jumped right into it.

"I met with Lily," I started. I looked between each of them and then continued. "First off, she's definitely our sister. Her and Blossom could pass for twins. The only thing she's missing is the natural hair we rock."

"Eww, she perms her hair?" Lilac asked, gagging.

"Hey!" Daisy exclaimed. "We don't judge people for how they wear their hair."

"Right, sorry."

"Anyway...this isn't about Lily per se. It's more so about what I learned from her." I felt myself getting nervous. Maybe I should have let Lennox come over after he was done teaching his class to do this with me. He offered a million times, and I turned him down because I thought I could do it alone. But what if they had the same reaction as me later? What if...

I shook my head and blurted it out. "Gerald...our father is dying. He's on life support." I glanced at each of my sisters, and they all wore different expressions that were hard to read. Instead of asking how they were feeling or what was going through their minds, I kept quiet.

"I'm not sure how I feel about that," Lilac murmured. "I mean..."

"Fuck him," Blossom blurted. "I hope he suffered."

"I'm with Blossom," Juniper chimed in. "I guess that's one less conversation I need to have."

Daisy stayed quiet. Her eyes were downcast as she fumbled with her fingers. My sister was an empath through and through. She picked up on our energies often, and sometimes it weighed heavily on her. She looked up and cleared her throat.

"Was that all we needed to know?" she questioned. I nodded, and she stood. "I have an early morning, so I'm going to head home. Could you send Lily's number in the sister group chat?" Instead of responding, I stood and walked her to the door. Before she could get away, I pulled my sister into a tight hug and rocked us from side to side.

"Call me later," I whispered into her ear.

"Maybe tomorrow. I need some time to process what I'm feeling." She pulled away and looked at me with a tiny smile plastered on her face. "I'll be alright, Mags."

"I know... I just—"

"It's okay," she murmured. "They need you more, especially Lilac. Blossom and Juniper are alright, but Lilac will struggle with this." Daisy kissed my cheek and sauntered off to her car.

"I love you," I called out to her.

"I love you more." I stood in the doorway and watched her drive off.

"We are going to head out too," Blossom announced with Juniper in tow.

"I rode with her."

"Are you guys sure?" They both nodded and kissed my cheek as they passed me. "You know that if you need me—"

"We're big girls now, Mags," Juniper called out, turning around to face me. She walked backward as she spoke. "Sometimes, we have to deal with things how we see fit, and I'd rather forget about the man then dwell on him, but I would like to meet my sister, so don't forget to send that number." Blossom blew a kiss and then slipped into the driver's seat of her truck. Juniper was in next, and then they were gone. I stepped back into my townhome and shut the door.

"Is it weird that I feel sad about this?" Lilac asked, startling me. I had no idea that she was standing behind me. "I mean, he abandoned us, so why should he deserve my sadness?"

"Someone helped me understand that my sadness wasn't for him, it was for the inner girl that got to experience him."

"Sounds like some shit Lennox would say," she joked. I smiled at the mention of him. "Oh, man. You're falling hard."

"I am, and it feels really good."

"I'm happy for you, Mags. You deserve to finally be happy. To be loved."

"So do you, Li." I pulled her into my arms, and she chuckled.

"Don't get all sentimental on me. I'll be okay."

"Are you sure because—"

"I'm positive. The girls are right, you know?" I lifted an eyebrow, and she elaborated. "You worry so much about us that you haven't really been living for yourself."

"I've been living," I argued.

"Your definition of living and mine are two totally different things, but right now, you have the opportunity to change that. Let that man give you some good dick and love on you." I rolled my eyes but still smiled at the thought of being dicked down again by Lennox. "See, you're thinking about it. Call him and get yours."

"I think I'll do that."

"Good, and while you're at it, set up a time and day for us to meet him. I think it's time."

"Yeah, me too," I agreed. Lilac wrapped her arms around me and sighed.

"I love you so much, Mags."

"I love you more." We stood in front of the door hugging for what felt like hours but had really only been a few minutes. Eventually, we broke our embrace, and Lilac headed out. After watching her pull away in her truck, I was alone with one thing on my mind.

Me: *Come over. I miss you.*

Me: *I need you. Want you.*

Lennox: *I'll be there soon, beautiful.*

I smiled and headed toward my bedroom to take a quick shower.

As I stripped out of my clothes and stepped into the shower, I thought about what my aunt said. I hadn't realized how attached I was to taking care of my sisters in situations like these. It was obvious after tonight that they didn't need me babying them anymore. I wasn't sure how I felt about that, but what I did know was that I was willing to back off if that's what they needed. It was time I focused on my own needs for once.

Lennox.

He'd won me over entirely after my outburst last night. I'd never seen someone so calm and understanding with me. In the past, my significant others would tell me that I was too much or too closed off. I was never enough for my partners. I didn't give enough, I didn't require enough. There was always a reason why those situations ended. And here Lennox was getting me in rare form, and he handled it like a pro. He made me see past my hurt. He made me...

"Why wasn't your front door locked?" For some reason, his

voice hadn't startled me. I felt him before he spoke. I slid the shower door back and eyed him. "Don't look at me like that." He was stepping out of his clothes before I could respond.

"Like what?" I asked, moving closer to the showerhead so he could step inside.

"Like you want this dick." My eyes immediately focused in on his chocolate erection. It was pointing straight at me, and I felt honored to have been picked by it.

"I do. I want it really bad. Can I have it?" I licked my lips and reached for his dick, staring in his eyes as I slowly stroked him.

"Take what's yours," he murmured.

"It's mine?"

"Mmhm," he hummed, falling onto the bench inside the shower and then snatching me into his lap. "Ride your dick, Lia."

Biting down on my lip, I lifted my body slightly, and he helped guide me down onto him.

"Fuck!" we groaned in unison.

"We should... We don't..." I paused and tried finding the right words. "We aren't using protection again, and I'm not on birth control." His dick was already deep inside of me, and now I wanted to bring up protection.

Great timing, Mags.

"I don't know what's up with me, but I keep wondering what it'll be like if I just purposely got you pregnant." He gripped my hips and lifted his pelvis to deliver one of his soul-stirring strokes. "Don't speak, just listen to my inner thoughts being spoken out loud."

"Oo-okay," I moaned, meeting his next stroke. Deciding to take over, I pressed my hands into his chest and bounced up and down on him, letting our contact echo through the enclosed space with joy. "Let me hear it, baby."

"What if we... F-fuck..." He paused as I twirled my hips at the tip of his penis and then dropped down onto him repeatedly. Lennox gripped my waist to stop me from moving. "What if we say fuck it and have a baby? I could cum in you tonight and every night after until you birth a Clarke. Can you see that with me, Lia? Because I can damn sure see that with you."

"A baby," I murmured, slowly rotating my pelvis. He couldn't keep me still even if he wanted to. I needed to feel this. I needed to feel him massaging my insides. While I rode him with conviction, I thought about his question. Could I have a baby with Lennox right now? Was I ready for that commitment? It seemed so soon, but truthfully, I saw so many things with him that I'd never seen with any other man. I saw a future with him. A life together for years to come. But one thing was for certain, and two things were for sure: I'd never settle for being someone's baby mother. Not even the man who had won the key to my heart fair and square.

"When I'm your wife... When I'm a Clarke, I will give you as many babies as you'd like."

"Yeah?" he asked, grinning at me like a fool in love. "Marriage is an option?"

"Mmhm, it's an option. A lifetime with you is an option."

Lennox lifted us from the bench, tilted my body back, and buried himself deep inside of me over and over again until I was shaking violently in his arms. He was digging so deep that by the time my orgasm had begun to subside, another one was hitting me just as hard.

"Swallow," he choked out, removing himself from inside me. I fell to my knees with one hand between my thighs, rubbing on my sensitive clit, the other stroking his dick until it was shooting cum onto my lips and then my tongue. "Fuck."

I used the tip of his penis to rub in the semen, and then I licked it off after sucking him completely dry. Lennox pulled me up from the shower floor and smashed his lips into mine. I was shaking with pleasure. He didn't care that I'd just had his nut all over my mouth. He was kissing me like it would be the last time. Our tongues were tangled together in the most beautiful way possible. He was making love to my mouth after fucking me into submission. This...this was something that I could get used to.

FOURTEEN

LENNOX

Two Weeks Later...

"Professor Clarke, you know what today is, right?" I chuckled and leaned into my desk. "We get to ask you whatever we want, and you have to answer us honestly."

"Are we at that part of the semester already?" I asked, running my hand down my face. I liked to give my students one thing they want halfway through the semester. Apparently, I was known as the mysterious professor, and everyone wanted to know more about me. So here I was, obliging their request to ask me one question each, and I vowed to be honest no matter what. "Alright, who—"

The door to the lecture hall opened and in walked Magnolia. Her eyes lit up when they landed on me, and I couldn't help but look her over as she moved toward an empty seat on the far right side of the room. She was rocking a long peacoat, but I knew her attire because I got to see her before she left my place this morning. A white blouse, black high-waisted skirt, and a pair of heels that added more than a few inches to her already long frame. Her heels clicked against the floor, and it was the only sound that could be heard. She'd made good on coming to see me, and I can't lie, I was feeling like I'd won.

"Alright," I blared, winking at Magnolia and then giving my attention to the rest of the room. "Who wants to go first?"

"I heard one of the other English professors saying that you're an author, is that true?"

"How many of you heard that and then went searching online for some of my work?" About half the room had their hands up, and I laughed. "Bunch of nosey ass young adults." Laughter filled the room, and I nodded. "It's true."

"But I didn't find anything that you've written," the same student who asked the question spoke.

"You already got your question, Ms. James. Next."

"Why can't we find any of your work?"

"I write under a pen name," I answered, cutting my eye at Magnolia. She had this small smile on her face, with her eyes trained on me and me alone.

"What's your pen name?"

I hesitated for a second. That was a question I didn't want to answer, but I'd made a promise. However...

"I'll tell you guys, but under one condition." A few spoke while others nodded their heads for me to go on. "This Sunday, I'm hosting a poetry night at Booker's Bar & Grill, and those of you who show up will get a free copy of my book and extra credit points toward your final grade."

"You had me at extra credit," Jacob Jones joked. More than half the class agreed, and I was pleased with their cooperation. I had planned on asking at the end of the period, but they made it easier for me.

"Alright, Parker Vincent."

"As in...the Parker Vincent?"

I shrugged. "I'm not sure what that means," I said, glancing around the room.

"There's only one Parker Vincent that's a New York Times best-selling author, Professor Clarke."

"I am him...he is me."

"Holy shit! You're famous, and we didn't even know."

"I'm a regular guy who is less than ten years older than most of you."

"Sounds like you're young and famous then to me," Lily Fredericks spoke. "I have a question, Mr. Clarke."

"Ms. Fredericks," I said, probing her to go on. My eyes moved around the room and then landed on Magnolia. I thought she'd still be focused on me, but she wasn't. Her head was craned to the side as she tried to see behind her.

"Are you seeing anyone?" I snapped my head in Lily's direction. She was sitting two rows behind Magnolia on the left side. "I'm only asking because you keep glancing at the pretty lady in the front, and I'm also sure I wasn't the only one thinking it." I looked at Magnolia, and she was eyeing me curiously. Almost in a 'you better not fuck this up' way.

"I am seeing someone, and she just so happens to be sitting in the front row."

"Are you guys in love?" someone asked. At this point, keeping my eyes off Magnolia wasn't an option.

"Yeah, I love her." I expected to see shock, but instead, I saw the response to my words in her gaze. *Yeah, she loves me too.* Her lips quirked up, and then she glanced down at the small table in front of her.

"Do you plan on marrying her?"

"One day," I said, "Let's move on, people. You're going to run her away."

"I don't know, Mr. Clarke," Lily said. "She looks pleased." I cut my eye at Magnolia, but she was watching Lily again. I frowned but looked away. I couldn't ask the question that I wanted without including forty-nine other people in my girl's family business, but I was almost positive this Lily was *her* Lily. I decided to cut the class short.

"How about this," I started, moving around my desk to take a seat. "You guys get out early today, and we pick up where we left off on Monday." No one answered, but bodies started moving. Minutes later, the lecture hall was empty, leaving Magnolia and me alone. I stood from my seat and moved toward her. As I slid into the spot next to her, I reached for her hand.

"That was her, huh?" She nodded and smiled.

"Yeah... I had no idea she was in one of your classes, but she did say she went to Penn."

"Small world," I murmured, kissing the back of her hand. "You look beautiful."

"You saw me this morning."

"Doesn't change the fact that you're still fine as hell."

"What's this about a poetry night on Sunday?" she asked, turning her body to face me. She crossed her legs and exposed a little of her toned thigh. I licked my lips and slid my free hand up her skirt. "Lennox—"

"I was going to bring it up to you later today. One of my good friends from college owns the bar, and he's letting me take it over for the night. I was hoping you'd accompany me."

"Can I bring my sisters, or is this a school thing?"

"Definitely bring them." I gripped her unexposed thigh and leaned in to kiss her.

"Oop—sorry." Magnolia and I both snapped our heads in the direction of the lecture hall door. Lily stood there with wide eyes. "I, um... I was waiting for Magnolia to come out and—"

"What's up?" Magnolia asked. Lily glanced at me and then back at Lia. "It's alright, he knows everything."

"I wanted to know if you spoke to the other girls yet. I've talked to them individually but—"

"They'll be at Booker's this Sunday," Magnolia cut in, smiling. Two weeks had passed since Magnolia's first meeting with Lily. The girls had been working out if they wanted to go see their father but ultimately decided against it. From what Magnolia told me, his fiancée was pulling the plug on him one week from today. They hadn't informed Lily yet about their decision, but I was positive they'd do it soon. "So, I hope you planned on showing up for extra credit."

Lily smiled and nodded.

"I mean, I don't really need it, but I love poetry, and I want a copy of that book." She looked between the two of us and added, "You guys are really beautiful together." And with that, she back away and then left the room.

"Now that I've really taken her in, she does look a lot like Blossom."

"It's so weird because Blossom looks the most like our mom, and I look the most like Gerald," she replied, turning to face me. "It's like a piece of my favorite lady found its way to Lily. Does that sound crazy?"

"It doesn't." I leaned in to make up for the kiss that was interrupted. I wanted to savor the moment, but we were in an open classroom that anyone could walk into at any time. Being on my best behavior was a must. "I'm glad you came here."

"Me too. I was on my way home, and then I figured why not show up like I said I would?" She pushed a finger into the right side of my cheek and laughed. "I've wanted to do that since the first time you smiled at me."

"Don't tell me that's going to be an ongoing thing."

"I can't confirm or deny."

I shook my head and went in for another kiss. "Let's get out of here," I mumbled into her mouth. "There's another class that comes in at eight."

"I never understood those super late classes. Wouldn't catch me in one."

"Me either. I was an afternoon class kind of a guy."

"No Fridays," we finished in unison.

Laughing, I gathered my things, hooked my bag onto my shoulder, and then reached for her hand.

"Where'd you park?" I glanced at her just as she pointed to the parking lot in front of us. We walked hand in hand and in silence the whole way. Once we approached her car, she turned her body to face me and leaned against the driver's side door.

"Did you mean what you said?" I was waiting for that question to come. "It's OK if you were just saving me from further embarrassment."

"Do you take me as a man who would tell a group of mostly twenty-one-year-olds that I love someone just because?"

"Well...no." Her gaze flickered around the parking lot and then settled back on me. "I guess I was just making sure."

"You guess?"

"I-I was making sure," she stammered. "I want to be sure that you are."

"I'm sure that I love you, Magnolia." I pressed my hands at each side of her face and then moved in closer. "I love you."

She bit down on her lip for a few seconds and then said, "I love you too, Lennox."

"Yeah?" Her response was a nod, and then she sealed her confirmation with a kiss.

"Don't hurt me," she muttered into my mouth. "I can't take—"

"Don't speak hurt into existence. I won't ever do anything to intentionally hurt you, Magnolia." I pulled back slightly and ran my fingers across her bottom lip. "You have my word. Now get in your car, drive safe, and call me when you've made it home, so I know you kept up your end of the bargain."

"I can do that."

The smile that stretched across her face tugged at my heart. Damn.

I was really in love again, but it felt different this time.

It felt *right*.

"I HAD no idea this would be the turnout," Devin said, glancing around his bar with a satisfied smirk on his face. I followed his gaze and nodded. I was impressed with the turnout as well. I'd extended an invitation not only to my senior class but my freshman class, and the other English professors and their classes. They, in return, offered their students extra credit if they showed up. Who knew a little boost in your grade would cause this?

"Hi, Professor Clarke," a group of girls called out as they passed. I nodded in their direction and then focused my attention on the door.

"Did the women look like this when we were in undergrad?"

"I haven't been paying attention," I said, laughing. "And you better be careful because some of these girls in here are just hitting eighteen."

"Sounds like a legal age to me," he mused. "But it would make me a creep, so I'll take heed to that. Actually, let me make sure my bartenders understand to check for their wristbands before selling them drinks." He stalked off, and I moved toward the left side of the bar.

"Professor Clarke!" I spun around and came face to face with the sixth flower sister.

"Lily," I said, nodding. "Glad you could make it."

She nodded and looked around. "Truthfully, I'm just here to meet my sisters. But I wanted to apologize for putting you on the spot in class on Thursday. I just wanted to know more about Magnolia."

"I didn't take..." My voice trailed off as I caught sight of Lia. I stepped around Lily after saying excuse me and moved quickly toward the front of the bar. I took in Magnolia as she looked around the bar and spoke to one of her sisters. She was wearing dark jeans with a red sweater, and a pair of red thigh-high boots. Once again, I was sucked into how fine this woman was, and she wasn't even trying. Her sister, Blossom, whispered into her ear and then pointed in my direction. Seconds later, our eyes connected, and her lips rose into a bright smile.

"Wassup, beautiful," I said as I neared them. "Hello, ladies." I glanced at each of them, but ultimately, my gaze returned to Magnolia. One of her sisters stuck her hand out in between us to gain my attention. She was the shortest of the five, but from the pictures I've seen, I knew her to be Juniper.

"I was wondering... Oh, I'm Juniper, by the way." And I was right. She held out her hand again, and I took it. After a few seconds, she pulled her hand back and smiled. "So anyway, I was wondering if you have a brother whose voice is as deep as yours or deeper?" Magnolia groaned, and I laughed.

"I do have a brother, but he's married with five kids and one on the way."

"One on the way," she mused. "That means he's happy. Welp, that was the only question I had for you. As long as you treat my sister right, then we won't have any problems. I'll be at the bar."

"Please, don't mind her, I'm—"

"Daisy." Her eyes widened as she nodded. "Your sister said you're the soft-spoken one."

"How do you know I'm not the soft-spoken one?" Lilac blurted, tilting her head at me. I didn't need her to be introduced to me to know.

"Because Daisy here already confirmed that she was who I thought, and I've already met Blossom."

"Mmph," she huffed. "Alright, then. I had it in my mind to give you a hard time, but you supposedly nailed my sauce recipe, and that's enough for me to give you a chance. You hurt my sister, and I hurt you." Lilac looped her arms with Daisy's, and they walked away, whispering to each other.

"It's nice to see you again, Lennox," Blossom murmured before sauntering after her sisters. Magnolia grabbed my face and planted an unexpected kiss on my lips.

"What was that for?"

"For being so amazing, and it's my apology. They were easy on you just now, but trust me, they are just getting started."

Laughing, I threw my arms over her shoulder and guided us toward the table Devin had blocked off for us.

"I was hoping Lily would keep them occupied," I said, sliding into the booth after her.

"Is she here already?" I pointed to the bar, and Magnolia looked that way. "Ah. She found them before they found her. I should probably—"

"You should sit back and chill with your man. I think your sisters can handle themselves."

"My man," she murmured, lacing her fingers with mine. "I like hearing that."

"Get used to it."

"Aye, Professor Ivy League!" Devin blared, walking up to our table. He glanced at Magnolia and then held his hand out to her. "I'm Devin, and you must be Magnolia."

"I am," she said, using her free hand to shake his. "This is your place, right?"

"How can you tell?"

"I'm good at reading people, and Lennox may or may not have put me up on game before I got here." Devin laughed and gave me a subtle nod of approval. "It's really nice in here."

"You'll have to come when it isn't full of college students."

"I'm sure my sisters will be back," she said, glancing past him. Devin turned his head and then looked back at us with a big ass smile on his face. The girls were making their way over, and I had a feeling he was banking on introductions.

"This place is super dope," Blossom said, sliding into the booth next to Magnolia. I'd noticed that she's the most attached to Lia. With her being the youngest, I wasn't surprised. She slid a drink to Magnolia, who picked it up and took a sip.

"Lennox, you know the owner, right?" Daisy asked, glancing at Devin. "Oh. I'm sorry, did we interrupt you guys' conversation?"

"No need for the apology," Devin said, holding his hand out. "I'm Devin. Lennox and I went to Villanova together, and I'm also the owner of this establishment."

"You have a nice place here," she said, taking his hand and smiling.

"Devin," Magnolia started. "On your left is Lilac and Juniper.

And this pest over here is Blossom." Devin shook hands with each sister.

"So you weren't lying when you said they were all named after flowers," he said, smirking. He opened his mouth to say something, but then Lily appeared from behind him. He glanced at her quickly, but when she took a seat, his gaze found hers again, and he stared. Gone was the smirk he was once wearing. I couldn't place the look currently on his face. I glanced at Lily, and she also had her gaze on his.

"Why is he staring at me like that?" she asked. The thing was she didn't take her eyes off him.

"I think he just fell in love," Daisy murmured, laughing.

"Well... Devin, this is Lily."

"Lily," he repeated. "Another flower."

"Yup, another flower," she replied, smiling. Devin nodded and then slowly turned his head to face me.

"Nox, you should probably address the crowd so we can get this thing started." He then walked away without another word.

"Awkward," Lilac mumbled. But then it was like nothing had happened. The girls started talking and asking Lily questions. This was their first meeting as a group.

"Is he OK?" Magnolia whispered in my ear.

"I have no idea, but I'll find out," I answered, kissing her forehead. "I'll be back." I removed myself from the table and headed in the direction Devin had walked in. I found him at the end of the bar, talking to one of his employees. He spotted me and nodded. After a few seconds, he turned to address me.

"Don't ask," he said.

"No can do. What was up with that?"

"I thought you said there were only five of them."

I eyed him curiously and then said, "When I told you that, there was only five. Now it's six." I shrugged and didn't elaborate. "You felt something?"

"The weirdest shit ever."

"Well, she's legal legal," I said, slapping his back.

"Man." He shook his head and then pointed to the stage where the DJ booth was stationed. "He has a microphone up there for you."

"This conversation ain't over," I said, backing away from him. I shook away my concern about Devin and hopped up on the stage. I spoke briefly to the DJ and then tapped the mic. The lights lowered on cue, and I began to speak.

FIFTEEN

MAGNOLIA

"Lily, you get to see Lennox twice a week, how is he as a professor?" Lilac asked, leaning into the table. I shook my head and sipped on the Long Island iced tea that Blossom had brought me. They'd been bombarding the girl with a million questions, but she didn't seem to mind.

"Everyone loves him," she said. "He's really laid-back but tough too. I guess it's a good balance because people fight to get into one of his classes. He has a waitlist sometimes. There are some praying that someone drops out so they can slip in."

That made me smile. After sitting in his class on Thursday, I had gotten the impression that he was loved by his students. He had this chill air about him that drew you in. Come to think of it, he had that same air about him when he wasn't in the classroom. Lennox was just an overall cool dude that was easy to love.

"I get good vibes from him," Daisy said, smiling at me. "He's definitely in love with you. I saw it in the way he looked at you when we first walked in. It was like his heart started beating again when he spotted you."

"I agree with Daisy," Blossom co-signed. "He loves you. I saw that the day he came to your place, and I was there."

"Yeah, I love him, too," I whispered. They all stared at me, and I just smiled. "I know it's soon, but—"

"That is not why we're looking at you," Juniper said, waving me off. "It just feels good to actually hear you say you love someone other than us, our New York girls, and Lori." We called Nova, Brynlee, and Elena our New York girls sometimes.

"And it's not too soon," Lilac added. "I don't think there's a timeframe on when you should love someone. It could happen two days in or two years in, but at the end of the day... Love is love, and that will never change."

I knew they were right.

I felt it in my soul.

Lennox was mine.

My love.

My *first* love.

The lights dimming and Lennox's deep voice filling the packed bar pulled my attention to the stage. He was standing in front of the DJ booth, looking handsome as ever. My heart beat against my chest with every word he spoke, and he wasn't speaking directly to me. At least, at first he hadn't been.

"First, I want to say that I'm grateful you all showed up tonight, even if you were bribed with extra credit." The room erupted in laughter, and I smiled. He had to know that they would have come even if a bribe wasn't given. *"Also, thank you to those who signed up to take the stage. If you're in my Monday and Thursday night English class, I have what I promised. Now, onto that other promise of mine, I have a piece prepared to start the night. I hope you enjoy it."*

"Oh, shit," Blossom whispered. "He does poetry?"

"You didn't tell us the man wrote poetry," Juniper said, turning completely in her seat. The rest of the girls were quietly staring at the stage, waiting for him to begin. I couldn't speak. He didn't tell me that he was participating, and now I was anxious to hear what he had put together.

"Wait... Magnolia, you didn't tell them he writes books?" I cut my eye at Lily, and she covered her mouth. "Oops." Their eyes were on me again, but I ignored each of them and kept my gaze trained on Lennox. He removed his phone from his pocket, swiped across the screen, and then held the mic up to his lips again.

"I wrote this six months after encountering the most beautiful woman I'd ever seen. It's short, but it's exactly what ran through my mind at that moment. I call it *Magnolia*," Lennox said, clearing his throat. "Here goes..."

> *Magnolia*
> *I figured out my new favorite flower today.*
> *I thought I knew it.*
> *I could spot the bloom from miles away.*
> *But there you were,*
> *Standing in front of me and rare as can be.*
> *Skin dark as coffee,*
> *And calling out to me.*
> *Your thick lips were coated in a purple gloss,*
> *Leaving the thought of kissing you deep in my thoughts.*
> *You graced me with your beauty today,*
> *And held out your hand for me to shake.*
> *That was all my heart could take.*
> *I figured out my new favorite flower today.*
> *Magnolia*

The room broke out into a series of finger snaps, but I couldn't move. Our table was eerily silent, and it hit me that we were all in shock. He'd written a poem about me, and it was fucking beautiful.

"I... Wow," Daisy whispered, breaking the silence.

"That was so damn beautiful," Lilac murmured, wiping her eyes.

"He said you're his favorite flower, Mags," Blossom cooed, kissing my cheek. "I guess I can share you."

I heard them, but my eyes... They were trained on Lennox,

and his were on me. He hopped off the stage and handed the mic over to Devin. This time when the tug in my heart began to intensify, I stood to meet him. We moved toward each other in a fluid motion. The noise and the people around us began to disappear the closer we became.

"Hey," he muttered, reaching for my hand to pull me into an embrace. He tucked a thick loc of hair behind my ear and kissed my cheek.

"You wrote a poem about me," I said, staring up at him. "And it was beautiful, Lennox. I don't even..." Instead of trying to find the right words, I cupped his face and pressed my lips gently to his. I kept in mind that his students and colleagues were still around us and pulled back after the quick peck. "Would it be bad if we left?"

"Give me a minute to make a few rounds, and then we can leave." I nodded and wrapped my arms tightly around his body.

"I love you, Lennox."

"I love you too, beautiful," he assured. "Don't ever forget it."

How could I?

Forgetting wasn't an option at this point.

Lennox had proved himself to me.

He'd shattered the wall in front of my heart and then politely asked for the key to remove the chains from around it. He deserved every part of me and I him.

Forty-five minutes later, Lennox and I were tumbling into his apartment, tearing each other's clothes from our bodies. I frantically fumbled with his belt buckle while keeping my lips connected with his. This moment was straight out of a romance movie, and I was the leading lady.

"Please," I begged, kicking my boots off and then assisting with getting my jeans down my legs. I need you inside of me." We moved quickly down the hall and then into his bedroom.

"Take the rest of that off," he ordered, tossing his shirt and boxers. I obliged his request and got rid of my thong and bra. I stood before Lennox naked as the day I was born. I threw myself onto his bed stomach first and positioned myself so that my ass was in the air and my face was planted deep into his comforter. "Damn."

"Mmm," I moaned, shaking my ass in his palm. "Smack it." He gave me a swift smack, and I yelped.

"You like that, don't you?" he taunted, repeating the move a few more times. He had no idea how much it turned me on. Lennox pressed his dick in between my wet pussy lips and slammed his way into me. When they say the first stroke is the best, believe them. My body responded immediately. I was shaking beneath him and whimpering for more. I gripped the blanket beneath us and began to meet his powerful strokes.

"Mmm, yes!" I wailed. "Yes. Yes. Yes."

"Fuck." Lennox gripped my hips and leaned his body forward. While digging deeper into me, he curled his fingers around my neck and forced my head back. With his lips pressed to my ear, he did the one thing that always sent me over the edge. He talked to me. He talked sweet to me. What man that's digging deep into a woman's guts whispers sweet nothings in their ear? My man, that's who. "You're so damn beautiful. My favorite sight to see on any day."

"Ooooh, L-Lennox." He picked up the pace and pushed me flat on my stomach.

"I love it when you say my name, Lia," he groaned. "Say that shit again."

"L-Len...baby, please." He stopped moving and pulled himself from inside of me. I rolled over onto my back and watched him through a hooded gaze. Lennox hooked one of my legs into the crook of his arm and then slid inside of me, reconnecting us. "Lennox."

"Mmhm. There it is." He smiled down at me and then bit into his lip. "Fucking stunning." Lennox resumed movement, burying himself deep inside of me with a smirk that revealed his deep dimple on his face. I knew our night had just begun.

"I DECIDED that seeing Gerald isn't necessary," I told Lennox as we laid in each other's arms. "I don't feel like seeing him will make me feel any different."

"How do you feel?"

"Like it's time to flip the page in my book and start a new chapter." I kissed his chest and tried burying myself deeper into his embrace. "You make me happy, baby."

"That's always the goal, Lia," he said. His voice was thick with sleep. Lennox had been forcing himself to stay awake because I couldn't sleep. We'd spent most of the night and morning having sex nonstop. I couldn't get enough of this man. I never wanted to. "Tell me if I'm ever failing at that."

"I will," I whispered, trying to blink back the sleepy haze that was suddenly accosting me. Lennox was rubbing small circles into my back, and that sped up the process. "I-I'm tired now."

"Good, let's sleep." I let my eyes close, and sleep took over with nothing but love on my mind.

LATER THAT AFTERNOON, I sat inside a restaurant with Lily and the rest of my sisters. Though I knew Lily was our sister, including her in the mix when I spoke of them was hard. We barely knew her. We were trying, but I was certain that each of us was having a hard time adjusting to the addition. Lily, on the other hand, seemed to be okay with our obvious discomfort at times. What I'd learned so far about her was that she just wanted to have a family outside of her mother. We could offer that to her, and she was fighting hard to achieve it. I could respect that.

"So, Lily," I called out. "We wanted to talk to you together so that this conversation doesn't need to be had again, and then we can move on with building a relationship with you."

"Okay," she murmured, pushing her glass away. She glanced between the five of us but ultimately settled on me.

"We know that you wanted us to see Gerald before his fiancée pulled the plug, but we've collectively decided that doing so isn't best for any of us."

Before poetry night, we sat down with each other and discussed how we wanted to move from here on. Everyone spoke their piece, and in the end, we came to the same solution. Healing didn't need to involve the person who hurt you. So while our father was a big part of why we hurt internally for different reasons, we made it our business to start seeking help in other ways.

"And," Daisy began. "We all understand that you got to see a side of him that we didn't, so don't feel pressured not to treasure that. The relationship we want to build with you doesn't have conditions. You can be who you are with us and feel how you want. There will be no judgment."

"Well, I am judging your choice to get perms, but other than that, we are a judgment-free zone," Lilac said, smiling. She was only partially joking, but again, Lily didn't seem to mind.

"Lilac, please stop," Daisy fussed, bumping her shoulder.

"Do you have anything you'd like to say to us?" Juniper asked.

"Just thank you," she answered. "For giving me a chance, even though I get perms."

"Hey!" Lilac blurted, tossing her hands up. "I was kidding." Lily gave her a knowing look, and they all began to laugh. I was quiet while they told Lily about the sleepovers that we hosted once a month. We were due for one soon, and she'd just received her permanent invite.

My thoughts were elsewhere. When I'd come to the decision that I wouldn't go see Gerald, it was because Lennox had helped me see differently. After allowing him and his love into my heart, I started to see that I could have healthy relationships without the fear of being left. It was that nagging feeling in the pit of my stomach that left me terrified of letting people inside. I could honestly say that the feeling was a mere pinch at the moment. It hadn't completely disappeared, but with time, I knew that it would. I was certain of that.

"Mags?"

"Mm," I hummed, glancing up at Daisy.

"Are you okay?" I looked around the table, and they were all staring at me with concern.

"Oh yeah, I was just thinking about—"

"Lennox!" they cooed in unison. And then the song began. "Lennox and Magnolia sitting in a tree, k-i-s-s-i-n-g. First comes love, then comes marriage, then comes a baby in a baby carriage."

"I don't know," I murmured, smiling. "The baby might come first."

"What?!"

EPILOGUE

ONE MONTH LATER...

"Are you sure I look okay?"

I glanced at my attire as Lennox and I exited his truck. After finding out that I was pregnant two weeks ago, we finally decided to make time to take the short trip to Jersey to see his parents.

There'd been a whirlwind of emotions, and Lennox was doing his best to protect my peace at all costs. I mean, he owed me since it's his fault that I'm getting fat. I knew after the night we had after the poetry event that I could possibly end up pregnant.

We were so wrapped up in the moment that we once again didn't use protection, and Lennox just kept shooting the club up after the first slip of the night. He figured it was a go big or go home moment, and I'd be lying if I didn't tell him a few times to give me his baby. What can I say? Good dick will have you doing and saying crazy things.

"You look beautiful, Lia," he answered, kissing my cheek and then lacing our fingers together. "As always."

"I feel fat," I whined.

"You aren't fat. You're carrying my baby, and the shit is sexy."

I bit down on my lip and pulled at the hem of my dress. "Repeat after me... I look beautiful."

"I look beautiful."

"I am not fat," he continued.

"I am not fat."

"I'm carrying a beautiful blessing, and nothing else matters."

"I'm carrying a beautiful blessing, and nothing else matters."

"I love Lennox."

"I love Lennox."

"I love you too, baby." He tugged on my hand, and we moved toward the door.

"You tricked me," I fussed with a smile on my face. He shrugged and winked at me.

God, I love this man.

Lennox opened the door to his father's house, and we walked inside. In a matter of seconds, a swarm of kids was on us.

"Uncle Lenny!" they shouted. "You're here." I couldn't help but smile at how excited they were to see him. It was obvious that my man was liked by adults and kids alike. I was quickly introduced to his three nephews, Cory, Ashton, and Omar. They gave me a onceover, said hello, and then took off running. It was his two nieces that stole the show.

"I'm Kendall, and this is Kaylie," the oldest of the two spoke. "Kaylie is his favorite, will you have a problem with sharing?"

"Kendall, take your grown ass into the playroom," Leonard, who I'd had the pleasure of meeting when he came to Philly on a business trip a week ago, yelled. Kendall took off running, but Kaylie stayed put. I let go of Lennox's hand and squatted down in front of her.

"I'm good with sharing, are you?"

"I like to share," she said, nodding. "Can I share Uncle Wenny with her, daddy?" She glanced at her dad, who nodded and laughed.

"Yeah, baby, you can share," he agreed. "Go ahead and go to the playroom." Kaylie took off running just as a very pregnant dark-skinned woman came waddling out from the back. I knew her to be Tamera, Leonard's wife.

"Oh, thank the Lord you're here," she praised. "I am starving, and that mother of yours wouldn't let any of us eat without you." She finally glanced my way, and her eyes lit up. "The pictures do you no justice. You're gorgeous."

"I feel so ugly," I said as we looped arms like we'd known each other our whole lives.

"Babies will make you feel that way, but I promise you're glowing," she said. "Take it from someone who is on her sixth and last pregnancy."

Tamera immediately made me feel like I belonged. The short walk to the kitchen had helped put my nerves at ease. It wasn't just about being pregnant—I was meeting Lennox's mother and father for the first time. After months of working through some things, their dad had finally moved their mother back into the home. This was the first time Lennox was seeing her since she'd been home, so maybe I was a little nervous for him too.

"The special guests have arrived," Tamera announced. Two sets of eyes landed on me, and I smiled.

"Oh my," his mother whispered. She had this timid way about her, but it didn't take away from her beauty. She was about five foot five with the same toffee-colored skin as Lennox. Her hair was long and wavy with a mixture of salt and pepper highlights. She smiled at me, and there was the dimple that Lennox had inherited.

"Hey, mama," Lennox greeted, gathering her into a hug.

"She's gorgeous," she murmured as they pulled away from each other.

"It's really nice to meet you, Mrs. Clarke," I said, stepping closer. "Lennox speaks very highly of you." She pushed my hand away and pulled me into a tight hug. I was a little shocked that she'd touched me. Lennox said she struggled with contact sometimes, but here she was hugging on me like I meant something to her.

"Call me Sia," she muttered into my ear. "And thank you for giving my son the one thing he's always wanted."

And then there were tears.

Stupid hormones.

A baby was something Lennox wanted so bad. He'd been denied the chance in his marriage, so when he found out I was pregnant, the man was near tears. He thanked me every day for a week.

"Alright, alright," his father chimed in with that gruff voice I was used to hearing over the phone. "It's great to have you here, Magnolia. Now let's eat." We moved into the large dining area where there was a feast laid out in front of us.

"Wow," I groaned, rubbing my stomach. Lennox chuckled and pulled my seat out for me. The kids were brought in and placed at a smaller table near us. Once everyone was seated, his mother spoke.

"Let's all join hands so we can bless the food." I linked hands with Tamera, who was on my left, and Lennox, who was at my right. "Father God, we thank you for bringing us together for this meal; may we continue to live in your friendship and in harmony with one another. Bless this food, a sign of your loving care for us, and bless us in our daily lives. Bless the babies with us and the ones to come. In Jesus' name, we do pray, Amen."

"Amen."

"Are you okay?" Lennox whispered in my ear. I nodded and threw a smile his way.

"I'm more than okay."

"I love you," he said, rubbing my barely-there stomach. "And you."

"We love you too."

As the food was served, I said a silent prayer of my own, thanking God for healing my heart enough that I get to experience this type of happiness. I never in my life thought I'd get to this point. Not where the urge to run didn't plague me on a daily basis.

With my head slightly bowed, I continued to give thanks. I thanked him for blessing me with Lennox. For bringing me closer to my sisters when it counted the most. For the growing child in my belly, and last but not least, I thanked him for providing me with the love I had always craved.

Not any type of love.

But a love that was created just for *me*.

A *perfect* love.

With a smile on my face, I pulled out my phone to send a text.

> Love is in the air, ladies. Who do you think will be next?

The End

AUTHOR NOTES

I hope you enjoyed Lennox + Magnolia's story. Please leave
Here are a few ways to stay connected with me:
Website: www.asiamonique.com
Like me on Facebook: http://bit.ly/AuthorAsiaMonique
Subscribe to my mailing list: http://eepurl.com/go_IYb
Join my readers group on Facebook: http://bit.ly/ForTheLoveOf-AsiaMonique
Follow me on Twitter & Instagram: www.twitter.com/_ayemonique